# JAMES PATTERSON
## BOOKSHOTS

Dear Reader,

You're about to experience a revolution in reading—BookShots.

BookShots are a whole new kind of book—100 percent story-driven, no fluff, always under $5.

I've written or co-written nearly all the BookShots and they're among my best novels of any length.

At 150 pages or fewer, BookShots can be read in a night, on a commute, or even on your cell phone during breaks at work.

I hope you enjoy *The Dolls*.

All my best,

James Patterson

P.S.
For special offers and the full list of BookShots titles, please go to
**BookShots.com**

# BOOK**SHOTS**

- ☐ *French Twist* (with Richard DiLallo)
- ☐ *The End* (with Brendan DuBois)
- ☐ *The Shut-In* (with Duane Swierczynski)
- ☐ *After the End* (with Brendan DuBois)
- ☐ *Diary of a Succubus* (with Derek Nikitas)
- ☐ *Detective Cross* (by James Patterson)
- ☐ *Private: Gold* (with Jassy Mackenzie)
- ☐ *The Lawyer Lifeguard* (with Doug Allyn)
- ☐ *Stingrays* (with Duane Swierczynski)
- ☐ *Steeplechase* (with Scott Slaven)
- ☐ *Nooners* (with Tim Arnold)
- ☐ *The Medical Examiner* (with Maxine Paetro)
- ☐ *The Dolls* (with Kecia Bal)

# BOOK**SHOTS**
*Flames*

# THE DOLLS

## JAMES PATTERSON
### with KECIA BAL

## BOOK**SHOTS**

Little, Brown and Company

New York  Boston  London

Copyright © 2017 by James Patterson

Hachette Book Group supports the right to free expression and the value of copyright. The purpose of copyright is to encourage writers and artists to produce the creative works that enrich our culture.

The scanning, uploading, and distribution of this book without permission is a theft of the author's intellectual property. If you would like permission to use material from the book (other than for review purposes), please contact permissions@hbgusa.com. Thank you for your support of the author's rights.

BookShots / Little, Brown and Company
Hachette Book Group
1290 Avenue of the Americas, New York, NY 10104
bookshots.com

First Edition: August 2017

BookShots is an imprint of Little, Brown and Company, a division of Hachette Book Group, Inc. The Little, Brown name and logo are trademarks of Hachette Book Group, Inc. The BookShots name and logo are trademarks of JBP Business, LLC.

The publisher is not responsible for websites (or their content) that are not owned by the publisher.

The Hachette Speakers Bureau provides a wide range of authors for speaking events. To find out more, go to hachettespeakersbureau.com or call (866) 376-6591.

ISBN 978-0-316-46977-7
LCCN 2016957125

10 9 8 7 6 5 4 3 2

LSC-C

Printed in the United States of America

# THE DOLLS

# CHAPTER 1

**IT SHOULD HAVE** been invigorating, jogging for the first time along Boston Harbor at dawn, breathing the cool briny mist.

But my morning run didn't work its usual magic.

A hot shower didn't help clear my mind, nor did the mug of green tea during my commute. I was trying to picture myself stepping confidently into a new job, a new city, and a new life. But all I felt was my stomach doing flips, over and over.

*At least my suit looks smart.*

I looked down at the crisp navy blazer, part of a steal I'd picked up in one of Chicago's consignment boutiques. I knew the color would work with my haircut, a shoulder-skimming auburn bob, in waves today, all part of an outfit planned—down to the pearl studs—months ago when I got the news.

But the shoes—the perfect nude pumps—were either left behind in Chicago, like the 24-7 crime beat, or squeezed into the bottom of one of the dozens of boxes I ripped open that morning, frantic and frustrated.

*Why didn't I keep the ensemble together in the move? Come on, Lana.*

Breathing in deeply, I picked up my pace in the final stretch of my trek from the T station stop to the office of the *Times-Journal*. This was it. *If I spend any longer waiting for courage to catch up, I'll be late.*

My first new job in a decade loomed just ahead, four stories of brick and glass outlined in the morning sun, taller buildings arching up behind it. I forced the anxiety fluttering up through my chest back down to the pit of my stomach. Another deep breath. I pushed open a glass door, taking a swift stride to a receptionist's desk.

The tired-looking woman behind it hardly looked up, but nodded knowingly when I introduced myself as the newsroom's new hire.

"I'll call Mr. Shawley to take you up," the woman said flatly, grabbing her phone.

Around the entryway walls hung poster-sized, front-page layouts in plastic frames. *That's where my byline belongs.*

The woman jammed the phone back into place, shook her head and stood, glancing at me. "Guess it's me who's taking you up. There's something going on."

"What is it?"

"Some kind of breaking news."

Maybe if the receptionist had been warmer, or if it had been any other day in my career, I would have tried for more information. I just followed, focused on not screwing this up.

The receptionist finished her chore as quickly as she could, letting a door slam behind her and leaving me in just a newsroom, which was sparse, even for 8:40 a.m. on a Monday.

*Where is everybody?*

There: a cluster of people behind a wall of windows on the opposite side of the newsroom. But there was a single reporter clicking at a laptop in a ghost town of waist-high cubicles. I recognized him from my interview as editor Tim Shawley. He looked in my direction and motioned me over.

"Welcome!" he said warmly. He gave a kind smile and stretched his sport coat over a barrel stomach. "So glad to be here." I smiled right back and gave a solid handshake.

"You're a little early—but that's good. We could use a crime-solver this morning, it turns out."

"Oh? Good. Well, I'm ready."

*That's a fib.*

He led me over to the glassed-in conference room and opened the door to a room full of half-finished mugs of coffee and the chatter I was used to in a busy newsroom.

"Guys, this is Lana Wallace. She comes from Chicago, where she's covered crime for the past ten years. She picked up a bunch of awards in that time, but I was able to convince her to make the switch to business—and the daylight shift."

The "guys" were about seven men in loosened ties—had they been here all night, or just gotten down to business and not tightened them yet?—and two women circling a whiteboard.

Tim introduced everyone and got back to business.

"We don't typically pull folks together for an editorial meeting this early, but in this case, we're trying to figure out how to deal with a high-profile murder—a second one, actually."

*Five minutes in—and it's a crime story. Bring it on.*

Elaine Hartman, the silver-haired city editor with a face full of stern lines, acknowledged me with a brisk nod and spun back around to the whiteboard.

"Katherine's just posted a breaking news update online with what we know from police and now the DA, which is little. Eric Blake, forty-seven, owner of several Boston-based companies, found dead in his condo late yesterday. Stabbing. Ruled a homicide." Elaine scribbled in black marker as quickly as she talked. "Katherine will also handle the press conference this afternoon. I think our editorial should focus on how the DA and police are being so damn tight-lipped. We've got a second homicide in the span of a week—and she's released a two-sentence statement to match the last two-sentence statement from police. Tyler found a headshot we had, but it would be nice if we could pull a little more info about Eric Blake. We've hardly said anything about who this guy is."

Tim glanced over the men thumbing through tablets on a table and turned to Katherine, pacing in flats around Elaine. Her brown hair was tied back in an efficient ponytail, a burst of curls bouncing behind her. I knew from her work bio and her history as a veteran crime reporter that she had to be mid-forties—but her energy level seemed more appropriate for twenty-two.

"What do we know about him?" Tim asked. "Any connections to Tony McAndrews?" And then to me, "He was the first victim, a private equity partner."

"Other than they were both loaded—not sure about the connection yet. Quick search shows that Eric Blake was the CEO of a startup called PrydeTek. I'm still checking our file stories to see what we've said about him before." Katherine paused, glancing at me. "Maybe we can have our new business reporter help me go through them?"

*Yes, please.*

Elaine studied my "pick me" face for a moment, then gave a quick response.

"That's fine. Maybe we can have her shadow you for now. Ed's on vacation, until next Monday. Trying to use it all up before he retires. The business section can wait a little longer for someone with…enthusiasm."

Katherine's expression was friendly, with a sparkle of mischief.

"Well, these guys both came from the startup sector. You could look at it as a business story—a business owner and a millionaire investor, both found tied up and slashed. *And* naked."

I took my cue.

"Right. We just don't know what kind of business they were up to."

Even Elaine broke her no-nonsense act for a second and chuckled.

# CHAPTER 2

***PENTHOUSE MURDER VICTIM*** *ID'd as Drex Equity Principal*
*Slain Business Leader Lauded for Tech Investments*
*Second Businessman Slashed*

I flipped through the headlines from last week—and this morning—on my phone while Katherine and I waited in a crowded reception area of the Suffolk County District Attorney's main office downtown. I was wedged between two irritated cameramen, equipment loaded over their shoulders.

"Where're you from?" one asked.

"Mack, this is Lana." Katherine looked back at me. "She's our new business reporter—only she's stuck spending the week with me."

I looked up from my phone with a smile at him.

"Some way to break her in," he grunted, as we were ushered to a law library set up for a press conference.

I hustled to get to a seat in the first of three rows of chairs that stretched from one book-lined wall to another. Mack and the other TV news crews set up their tripods in the back and strung them to eight microphones they attached on top of a wooden podium.

District Attorney Allison Brito, short and smart-looking, walked in moments later, and stood behind the microphones. She was flanked by men and women, including department leads from the Homicide Unit and the Special Prosecutions Unit that handles white-collar crime.

"That's Andre Davies with the Boston Police Homicide Unit—he's cool." Katherine finished announcing the lineup and her voice died down to a whisper, along with the din of gossip all around us.

The DA adjusted a few of the microphones, cleared her throat, and thanked the group for coming. The roomful of reporters watched expectantly.

In a span of about three minutes, she recapped the brief statement her office had sent to news crews this morning. "The investigation is ongoing. Please let the public know that anyone with information should call Boston Police or Crime Stoppers immediately. And, yes, investigators are looking into potential similarities to the previous fatal stabbing."

*That was it?*

There was surprise at how quickly the DA was done with her update. And then the questions started.

"What have you uncovered about last week's murder?" a woman's voice rang out.

"We are following up on every possible lead in the case of Mr. McAndrews."

"What about the medical examiner's report?" Another voice. And another question that went unanswered.

"Are there any leads on the suspect—persons of interest?" The same voice, a man, tried again.

The DA sighed, but answered: "Not yet. No witnesses that we know of. That's really all I can release at this time. We are trying to be sensitive to the families."

*Outrageous. A killer is at large—maybe two killers—and the DA's hardly saying anything.*

"Allison, can you at least tell us how many stab wounds?" This time, it was me, shouting over the crowd. "And where?"

She stopped her exit—and looked at me in the front row.

"Who are you with?"

"Lana Wallace, with the *Times-Journal*." I didn't let my voice waver.

The cramped room was quiet for a moment while she studied me.

"A single puncture wound to the chest. That's *really* all I can say."

And it was the last thing she said, walking away with a few bold reporters trailing her to the door. I would have, too, but Katherine had my elbow.

# CHAPTER 3

**DETECTIVE ANDRE DAVIES** was shaking his head—in a friendly, you-know-I-can't-say-anything way—before we got to him.

"Andre, this is nuts and you know it." Katherine cut right to the point. "Two weird murders in one week, two millionaires—and we're getting zero. I guess money talks."

The detective stayed composed, his strong jaw set, but his green eyes smiled.

He tilted his head—he was at least eight inches taller than Katherine and I—and in a lowered voice said: "Except, sometimes money doesn't talk."

He was talking to Katherine, but his eyes wandered to me.

"The families are difficult, I'm sure. And they have to be putting the pressure on to keep this quiet," Katherine answered quickly. "Is that why the DA took over media relations from Boston PD?"

Only a smile in reply.

Getting nowhere, Katherine switched gears and introduced me to Davies. I shook his hand, thinking *thank you, Katherine,* as she launched into small talk. "How are your boys doing?" she asked. "Did you and Kelly pick a preschool for Noah?"

*Damn. Of course. He's married.*

He relaxed.

"No on preschool, but one week into summer break for Justin and we've already visited the ER, so we're off to a running start. Don't let anybody tell you bowling's not a sport. It's a dangerous one." *Lucky Kelly. He's funny, too.*

"Lana, are you as much of a troublemaker as Kat here?"

I tried to think of something witty to say back, but I was at a loss.

"We get along so far, if that's any sign." That was the best I could do. I tried for a playful smile.

"You covered crime in Chicago? This should be nothing."

"Well, this is certainly different," I answered. "I mean—some guy fatally stabs a man in the chest and walks away. Nobody saw him? *Either time?* You guys have to know a lot more than you're saying. And what kind of motive? Is it the money?"

"Like Allison said, one stab wound. That means little spatter. Perp *could* have walked away without drawing attention. No prints showed up on the handles of either of the knives—"

"Where'd you find them?" I squeezed in a question.

"Still there."

"You mean…in the victims' chests?"

Detective Davies gave a barely detectable nod, and looked around. The room was empty now, besides the three of us. He whispered: "Deep, too, all the way to the handle. Horizontal, aligned with muscle grain. Means even less blood."

"Both times?"

One more nod. Finally, I was getting somewhere.

*Same MO. And the killer had to be strong—and calculating—to shove a kitchen knife that far, in the right place, in one hit.*

"Were there signs of forced entry?" I tried for more. "A struggle? And why were they naked?"

Amused by the barrage, the detective settled a melting gaze on me.

"I've said too much already—and nothing I did say came from me. It's nice to meet you, Lana. Welcome to Boston."

# CHAPTER 4

**I WAS MAKING** good time. Great time, actually.

By 7 a.m., I'd enjoyed a run on the Harborwalk, spent a half hour or so reading through the first draft of Kat's Sunday piece on the homicides—by her flattering request—and then was outside again. I'd abandoned my PowerBar for a leftover oatmeal cookie from Kat, the office baker. The tray Kat had brought in for everybody was enough to cover yesterday's afternoon snack and this morning's breakfast. I made a note to return the favor after I'd had time to unpack my own KitchenAid and unwind this weekend.

Oatmeal qualifies as breakfast in my book. Maybe not the chocolate chips. But it was time to celebrate, I decided.

So as I walked through the Seaport District, I dialed my mom back home in Charlotte, keeping a swift pace past one sleek condo project after another. I gave her the updates: my newfound friend, my own swanky high-rise apartment—a big splurge—and the homicide investigations.

"Baby, you sound so happy."

I knew she'd get it. Outside a newsroom, only my mom would see why a pair of murdered millionaires would have me going like this.

Maybe, if I could help fill in the holes—and there were still plenty of those—I could land one of those front-page bylines. It was time to find out a little more about Mr. Blake.

*Back in the game. God, it feels good.*

I didn't mention to her where I was going, though. I hadn't quite mentioned it to anyone else, either, though I had a feeling Kat would understand.

"Just be careful, sweetheart. I want you to get the story—you always do—but I also want you to be safe."

"I know, Momma. I love you. Lots."

I was almost there, Fort Point Channel shimmering before me, the skyscrapers rising up in the Financial District just over the bridge. The global headquarters for PrydeTek sat a few blocks ahead. It was just 7:20.

I thought a head start would allow me to pick up some ideas for sources before I made it into the office—hopefully with a clearer picture of murder victim number two. The research I'd done on PrydeTek had yielded surprisingly little information, for a startup that had generated a lot of buzz. Every story on the company mentioned that it was developing new technology for artificial intelligence, but there was a total lack of detail or information about the founder—Eric Blake.

*This is my chance. I'm going to own this story, whatever it takes.*

But the front doors of the office complex were locked. After a few moments, someone stepped up behind me.

"Oh, excuse me, sir." I stepped aside. "Do you work here?"

"It's Daniel, not sir, and I do."

He was young, under thirty I guessed, dressed in a button-up shirt with jeans and sneakers.

He didn't exactly look like a chief technical officer, but that's what he said he was.

"Who are you?" He unlocked the door and looked me over.

"A reporter with the *Times-Journal*."

That stopped him, and not in a good way.

"I'm not the crime reporter. The new business reporter. I'm just looking into the business side of the story. After Mr. Blake's…passing. What he left behind."

I had his ear.

"I'd hate for this to all be about how he died. I'd like to cover who he was, what he contributed," I said. "I want to tell a little more about the technology you're developing."

There's the trick. Ask an engineer about his firm's technology. He held the door open for me.

A woman, her head bent over her phone, was the only other person there.

"Marlene?" Daniel sounded surprised. "Oh, right, Elliott is in today for the meeting."

Marlene looked up through thick glasses and nodded to us before she padded down a hallway, still thumbing through her phone. She looked a little out of place in the contemporary surroundings, like she was meant to be behind the scenes.

Almost everything inside was white, from the matte paint along the corridors to the mid-century modern furniture—with the exception of a lounge, painted in saturated greens with bright-orange beanbag chairs over a black rug and an oversized, disco ball of a light fixture as a focal point.

Daniel and I sat in one of the conference rooms, which had whiteboards for walls. The desks were whiteboard, too, and all were written on, here and there: bullet-point lists, numbered tasks with names assigned, and a doodle or two. It seemed like a fun place to work, and Daniel said it was.

"What's best, though, is what we were all working toward. The subsidiaries were—are—successful. We've all really been pushing the limits. Ideas people said wouldn't fly. Stuff people said couldn't be developed—deep learning, modeled after the human brain, on a whole other level. We have commercialized working prototypes, with more advanced models in R&D."

I nodded along. As a business reporter, I'd listened to my fair share of visionaries and computer geniuses. Daniel was clearly drinking the Kool-Aid. He laid out Mr. Blake's mission for Pryde-Tek: to create useful, likable artificial intelligence, eventually in every home, as familiar as a PC. The company's breakthroughs, so far, included creating what Daniel called "advanced personality" beyond anything on the market or under development elsewhere: robots that could replicate and learn emotions, and respond to other people's emotions. Daniel described this capability in rapt terms.

I gently brought the conversation back to Blake. "What was Mr. Blake like as a leader? *His* personality?"

"Eric could be hard to work for," Daniel said. "He was demanding. The kind of guy who didn't take 'No.' But that's why we're doing what we're doing. He saw the benefits of artificial intelligence on a practical, everyday level. In those areas where he wasn't an expert, he'd hire someone who was. But if someone didn't live up to his expectations—or deliver what they promised—they had to go. He was the big-picture type."

"Are you one of those experts?" I wanted him to keep talking.

"My background is robotics," he answered. "MIT, mechanical engineering and computer science. Actually, I met Eric in the AI lab there."

"He knew how to build a team," I said. "What about his personal life? Family?"

Daniel bristled. I'd lost some footing.

"Not the kind of thing we talked about. He was all professional. No kids. I think he's married, or used to be. But, he just put so much into this company, so much time."

I nodded, and circled back to the tech.

"You said there are working prototypes. On-site?"

# CHAPTER 5

**THE LAB WAS** set up in warehouse fashion—a clean, sprawling space three stories high, with metal walls and wide windows on the third level that brought in sunlight. Between blocks of machines to the left and right were single-level glass rooms, with roofs and overhangs that looked to me like garage doors.

Daniel pulled a badge from a back pocket of his jeans and stopped in front of one of the rooms. Inside, furniture in vivid tones mimicked the colorful employee lounge out front. The glass doors slid open and Daniel offered me a beanbag.

"Say hi to Alex."

He watched my face for reaction and motioned toward a creature with metal, mechanical arms, legs, and feet, but a face shaped like a person's.

Alex stood up on a pair of rectangular feet, knees still bent, at the sound of its name.

I waved, speechless.

From the shoulders up, Alex looked like a child, about four feet tall—but with a light-tan, shiny plastic face and slightly oversized, round eyes. It wore a golf shirt and jean shorts. It even had hair—

straight and glossy brown—shaped in a little boy's haircut around its face.

"Hi, Daniel." It spoke in a child's voice, too. "Who's your new friend?"

I laughed.

*Cuter than I expected.*

"You think I'm funny?" Its tone was interested—not offended.

"I think…you're adorable."

The childlike robot's eyebrows raised and I heard it make a jubilant cry—like a real child who's just been told, yes, he really can have ice cream. His face shifted into a smile of delight, cheeks squeezing up at the corner of each eye.

I looked over at Daniel—and the robot followed my gaze, turning his head.

"Did you see that?" Daniel's arms were crossed, chest risen in pride.

"What part? See what?"

"He can actually visually process the suggestions your face is making—where you're looking, and also whether you're happy or upset—and react to those," Daniel answered, "with his own, learned emotions. Watch," Daniel said, then furrowed his brows and pinched his lips together tightly.

"What's wrong, Daniel?" Alex asked.

Daniel looked over at me.

"Don't you like her?" Alex's voice rose, in concern. "Does she make you worry?"

"Wow," I told Alex. "You're smart, too."

"Thank you…lady," Alex said, guessing my gender. "Daniel, what's this lady's name?"

I started to answer, but Daniel shook his head and raised both hands in my direction.

"Wait."

He led me just outside the door and whispered: "Tell him a lie. Make up a name—but make it believable. Try to convince him."

"Why?"

"You'll see. Just give it a try."

*Weird. But, okay.*

I stepped back into the room and looked at Alex. *He is way too cute.*

"My name is Rose." I gave my mom's name.

"Hmmmm." Alex looked at me, squinting his eyes, cocking his head, as if sizing me up.

"He knows," Daniel said. "He recognizes signs of dishonesty. Little things you do—your face, your body—that you don't even know you do. That's where it goes beyond machine learning. This is deep learning, deep neural networks—a mix of hardware and software." Daniel kept going. "It functions like the neurons in the human brain."

"But why a child?" I almost felt bad, asking in front of Alex. "I mean, if the goal is to create useful household robots?"

Daniel shook his head.

"Useful, *likable* robots," he said. "This prototype is more about the psychology—what makes us like them, or love them. Part of that is its capacity to feel and respond to your feelings. That's the brain side."

Daniel put his hand on Alex's head in an affectionate way.

"But there's a whole other side of its capabilities," he said. "Things like balance are more complex than you'd think."

Daniel pushed the chairs from the center of the room to a corner and walked over to Alex, who looked expectantly at him. With two hands, Daniel shoved him—hard.

*What the hell?*

"What are you doing?" I was shocked.

Alex stumbled sideways—almost falling, but not quite.

He regained his footing and looked at Daniel, who was looking at me. Then Alex's face copied mine: furious.

"It's okay," Daniel said. "Part of the testing. We're making gains here, breaking ground with what we can do."

Daniel hurried over to Alex again, and before I could say anything else, he lifted his foot and sent Alex stumbling again in the other direction with a powerful kick.

This time, Alex crashed into a wall and fell forward onto the floor.

"And he can get up—from the ground, too. Just takes a few seconds."

But in one second, I was there, kneeling beside Alex, who had his hands flat on the ground. I put out my hands, and he stopped, looking at my open palms, then up at my face. He wore a confused expression.

I moved to the front of his body, still holding out my hands.

"Put your hands on mine," I instructed. "You can push off of them to pull yourself up."

He still looked unsure, so I reached down and tried to put my hands under his. It felt like lifting one corner of a metal bed frame.

Alex was heavy, but I did it. One hand first. Then I had to wrap my arm around the steel structure and use my shoulder to lift his other side while I slid my hand under his. His weight smashed down against my palms on the polished concrete.

"Am I hurting you?" Alex's voice sounded worried.

"Empathy!" That got Daniel excited. "He feels sorry for you."

I ignored Daniel and pulled up, as hard as I could, trying to keep my back straight, like I was lifting a box of books. It felt the same.

His torso lifted slowly with the hum of gears cycling, until we were both kneeling on the floor, eye level.

From the corner of my eye, I saw Daniel standing, watching, like he wanted to take notes. Like this was another test.

Alex still had both hands—four fingers stuck together in a piece of plastic that bent at the knuckles and a thumb that moved independently—resting in my hands.

"What's your real name?" Alex stared at me, eyes open all the way.

"Lana."

"Thank you, Lana."

# CHAPTER 6

**IT TOOK THREE** rings at the bell before a brass handle turned on one of the antique double doors—painted in glazed red that popped against the creamy neutral stone exterior of the Victorian brownstone along Commonwealth Avenue.

A young woman leaned out of the entryway. With a chic messy bun and airbrushed makeup, she was the type of woman you'd expect to see stepping into the Cartier or Chanel shops I'd just walked past in Boston's Back Bay.

"Can I help you?"

"Are you Adrianne Blake?"

"Why?" She examined me, up and down, and then looked like she was waiting for bad news.

I knew this would be a hard sell.

"I'm a reporter" —the door started to creak closed again— "a business reporter, working on a story about your husband's contributions to the tech sector."

"I can't help you. Thanks."

She tried to shut the door but I did the pesky journalist trick from the movies and stuck my foot in it.

"I told you—I don't have anything to say."

"I'm sorry to bother you, at this time, especially," I said. "I know this all has to be really hard. I just don't want the impact of your husband's work to be lost in the stories about how he died."

Her face told me I was only making this worse.

She looked more angry than sorrowful, but I tried to work the "business impact" angle one more time.

"I spoke to the people at PrydeTek. I know about his developments, the advances they are making, and that your husband's contributions—"

"My *estranged* husband, please." I was surprised to see her open the door wider and lean against it. "He wasn't all he was made out to be. That's about all I have to say."

"I'm sorry. I didn't realize—"

"Yes, we were separated," she said. "It wasn't good, so if you're doing a story, I'd appreciate if you didn't mention me. At all."

"I can do that." I offered. "Could you spare ten minutes, though—just on background. I don't want to paint the wrong picture of Eric—Mr. Blake."

She rolled her eyes at his name, and motioned for me to step into a columned foyer that led to a sumptuously appointed living room. The Blakes had high standards, and it showed through every room, each one a study in shape and color. The design elements were clearly a point of pride for Adrianne, who happened to be an interior decorator. That's how she met Eric in the first place. When he was still married to his second wife, she helped him turn his office headquarters into his vision of a Google- or LinkedIn-style campus.

But I had a feeling she was trying to show me more than her eye for design.

By the time we reached the second level of the home, she had opened up about Eric Blake's trysts, as if she'd been waiting to vent. They'd only been married a year when Adrianne started to wonder about his late nights and weekends, she said. And she'd been right. It wasn't long until Eric had stopped trying to hide his habit of collecting new girlfriends, some of whom he even brought into their home while she was away with clients.

I followed her up another elaborate staircase—Adrianne was really going with the stories, marching up the steps with rage—and then she stopped inside the master bedroom, where a huge canopy bed almost took attention away from a grand fireplace, the fourth I'd seen so far. There was a lot of finery to absorb in this room, one Adrianne said she hardly visited—even though he had moved out, she said, there were too many bad memories in this one.

She stood before a set of closed closet doors.

"I knew about the other women and, to be honest, expected that," Adrianne said, hands on the knobs. "I'd been warned. I'd learned to deal with it the best I could. But this—this was *way* too much."

Considering the grandeur of the home tour, I wasn't sure what luxury to expect inside the closet. Something pricey, certainly.

But nothing could have prepared me for the spectacle behind those doors.

Centered between rows of silk and lace strung along the sides of a wide closet—a woman reclined on a chaise longue, wearing nothing aside from a choker of jewels that glittered in light from the bedroom.

Adrianne flipped a switch that illuminated the woman's face and bronzed body—an exotic beauty with eyes half closed, lying motionless on her side on the plush emerald velvet.

I didn't know what to say or think.

The woman's head rested against a side of the high-backed chair, legs stretched out gracefully across the length of it. She had smooth, dark hair that flowed down past her breasts, just grazing the narrow dip of her waist. Her hip and bottom rose up in a sensuous curve, the most dramatic of many contours of sun-kissed flesh.

After a moment to make sure she wasn't going to move, I couldn't resist stepping closer.

I looked at her face.

From the crescent of her almond-shaped eyes, long lashes extended over the top of high cheekbones. Her pink lips were just barely parted, plump, and perfectly glossed.

She was gorgeous. Like supermodel gorgeous.

*She has to be the most beautiful woman I have ever seen—in person. Or maybe ever, anywhere.*

"He called her 'Emily.'" Adrianne's words interrupted my thoughts.

"She's just *one* of them," she told me. "One of his more expensive dolls, too, at the higher end of the $750,000- to-million-dollar price tag. She's also the reason I kicked him out, finally. He moved her in here like she was a real person—like she was going to be a part of our relationship. Clearly he wanted to be rid of me. Why else would you do that? I just left her here because I feel sorry for her and I don't know what else to do."

*A doll.*

It was like looking at a living, breathing version of a magazine centerfold—except she wasn't living or breathing. I touched her cheek, warily. Soft as the velvet behind her. Then her shoulder and arm. Smooth, soft flesh.

"Doll?" I said aloud the word I couldn't stop repeating in my head.

I looked at Adrianne, stunned.

"*One* of them?" I asked.

There were so many questions.

She nodded, and I moved a lock of Emily's hair behind her shoulder, feeling it between my fingers. I thought I even smelled a delicate perfume—a blend of orchids and coconut, maybe.

"Careful—what did you say your name is?"

"Lana."

"Lana," she continued. "I don't know where the On button is."

I turned to Adrianne.

*On button?*

My mind circled back to the morning, my walk-through, the prototype. *PrydeTek's technological advances put to use…*

The skin on my arms tingled. Only the bottom half of Emily's glowing amber irises, edged in deep brown, showed beneath the sweep of her lashes—but I couldn't help feeling like the doll was watching me.

*This woman could walk and talk? And what else? And why?*

Mrs. Blake answered the question that had begun to shape in my mind before I could ask. I didn't want to ask.

"That's right, Lana. She can do everything a real woman can."

She nodded at the disbelief in my face and stretched out the syllables in the next word she spoke:

*"Everything."*

# CHAPTER 7

**MY MIND STILL** buzzing with questions, I didn't realize how hungry I was until my mouth watered at a bouquet of sizzling burgers, caramelized onions, and sautéed peppers.

After about all the technology my mind could process in one day, I had decided to take Kat up on her offer to meet for dinner at Mr. Bartley's Burger Cottage in Harvard Square. I skimmed through an almost overwhelming variety of seven-ounce burgers with names that were puns, heavy on the blue cheese and loaded with artery-clogging toppings, and settled on the "Fiscal Cliff," with onion rings.

"How did you make out today, Kat?"

Katherine sighed and settled back into her chair, sipping soda from a cafeteria-style plastic tumbler.

"I'm just not getting much of anywhere on the murders," she answered.

"Still nothing new from police?" I debated whether, or even how, to tell her about my adventures.

"No," she answered. "Talked to Davies today. They're looking at connections between the victims, potential money trails. Nothing noteworthy has turned up."

"Nothing at all?"

Then Kat grinned.

"Oh, yeah. One noteworthy item to report."

I waited and then gestured for her to keep going. "Well, what?"

"He asked me about you."

I laughed. "You tease."

I waited until we'd both enjoyed the first few juicy bites of burger before I went back to the murders.

"I made a little progress today, digging around on Eric Blake." I threw it out there, eyeing my friend for her reaction.

"Did you?"

She looked excited. *Thank God.*

"Who did you call?" she asked me.

"I went to his company's headquarters, and then his home—well, his former home. He and his wife had split."

"Look at you, knocking on doors. I told Tim you were a go-getter."

I couldn't hold back a wide smile. That was a compliment, from someone like Kat.

"What did you find?"

I told her about the little guy from this morning at PrydeTek—and the doll at my last stop.

"This is bizarre—I know—but I got the feeling she was watching me," I said, still processing the experience myself. "And I don't think she liked what she saw."

Kat's mouth dropped.

"Wait, wait, wait." She shook her head. "First, of all, who the hell wouldn't like you? And second, you mean—like—a *sex* doll?"

I shrugged my shoulders.

"I guess," I answered, lowering my voice. "That's what the wife meant, right? What else does a forty-something businessman need with a life-sized, naked doll sprawled out on a chaise longue, surrounded by lingerie?"

"Wow, talk about a skeleton in the closet." Kat couldn't resist the joke.

I chuckled, and Kat watched my face for a second.

"Had to be a weird day for you," she said.

"Weird, creepy, and maybe a little…sad, too," I said. "I know that sounds silly."

"No, it doesn't. Little Alex sounds lovable."

"I guess that's what they were going for—or 'likable,'" I said, thinking back to the engineer's description. "But can't they do the shoving-around testing on models that don't have emotions built in yet?"

"No kidding," Kat said. "That and the sex doll tell a lot about Eric Blake's character. What a hog. His wife wasn't enough. The other women weren't enough, so what does he do? He makes his own woman—one who can't say no."

We were quiet for a minute, people-watching. It was mostly students around us—groups of four or five sharing stories and a few solo, reading and sucking down iced tea or lemonade.

"So…did Emily spook you enough to get you to stop chasing down robots?" Kat asked.

"Hell, no. I think I'm getting somewhere," I answered, examining Kat's reaction for any hint of offense. "I just don't know where yet."

I finished the last of my onion rings, worry still gnawing at me. *Just ask her.*

"Kat, are you okay with me poking around on this story? I don't want to be wandering too far into your territory."

Kat gave me a "come on, girlfriend" look.

"We've got to get this story nailed down," she said. "This could be a good breakthrough story for you here. And somebody's got to keep the guys in the office on their toes. I'd prefer if it were my shadow for the week—my new partner in crime."

With a toast of our sodas, I had the green light.

# CHAPTER 8

*Sandra*

**AS SOON AS** she heard the key turn in the lock, Sandra slipped from the king-sized comforter's satin squares in a frantic race for the door. She straightened her powder-blue teddy over her hips and smoothed her hair in a full-length mirror near the entryway, ready to greet the person whose return she anticipated every day.

Allen was home from work.

Sandra was in her place, primped and pretty.

And he shoved right past her.

"Allen, you're home."

Trying to adjust to his mood, Sandra spoke cautiously to his broad shoulders.

"No shit." It was almost a grunt.

Allen slipped off his coat and tie, throwing them over the arm of a settee. He walked toward a liquor cabinet in the kitchen as he unbuttoned his shirt. Ice clinked in a glass as he poured a drink.

"You can give this to me." Sandra walked up beside him, carefully taking his shirt to hang in the closet and then picking up the coat and tie along the way.

She was standing by oversized windows when Allen came into the bedroom in his undershirt. He sank into a chair with a tumbler of scotch and polished off the last few swigs while Sandra stared outside, eyelids heavy with longing.

Behind the skyscrapers, the harbor shimmered in the pink-orange hues of dusk. She focused on the buildings and what she could see of the busy streets below. People looked like little dots, rushing down sidewalks. Cars and taxis lined up and zipped through streets like toys.

"Allen," she said, sweetly. "What's that building? The one with the gold shapes around the top?"

Allen grunted again, exasperated.

"Do we have to do this every single time?" he said. "You already know. Work was hell. This isn't what I'm supposed to come home to. I'm not up for this game of yours today."

"Yes, I know, but I want you to tell me what people do in there." She pressed both hands against the window.

Slamming his glass onto the dresser, Allen stood furiously. His belt buckle made a thud as it hit the thick carpet.

He grabbed one of her arms by the elbow, but Sandra yanked it back, not ready yet to let go of the pictures in her mind of women and men talking to each other, calling home and packing up from work to enjoy their families. She saw them in her mind on their way home, hurrying to gather around tables in TV commercial perfection—soaking up spilled juice with brand-name paper towels or slicing into chicken seasoned with a blend of Italian spices.

She'd been charging in bed for the past four hours so she could be ready for him, for what Allen wanted.

Maybe he would give her five more minutes at her favorite spot. Behind her, Sandra felt the swift kick against her knees. It knocked her flat on her back.

"I told you I'm not in the mood for this game today," Allen said, his face over hers. "You forget what you are. Go ahead and try to get up yourself, dumbass bitch."

Sandra didn't move. She wouldn't give him the satisfaction of watching her struggle to pull her body off the floor. Even if she could cry, she wouldn't have let him see it.

He jerked her up by both her arms until she was tottering on her feet, knees still bent.

Allen stood back, cleared his throat, and enunciated a command: "Sandra, hot talk."

It was the first time he'd said her name since he came home. It made her head shake, slightly, but activated the response Allen expected.

Sandra rose to standing, slowly. She turned her head to him with a sly smile, batting blue eyes under a headful of loose blond waves.

She pursed her lips in a small pout.

"*That's* what you want, baby." She walked a few steps toward him. "You want me to tell you how bad I want you?"

"Fuck, yes." His voice was more a rumble now.

Sandra put a hand on each of his shoulders and leaned in like she was going to kiss him.

Instead she gave him a little shove onto the edge of the bed.

"I've been thinking about you undressing me all day," her voice dipped to a whisper as she put her arms around his shoulders, her breasts hovering around his mouth.

"I want you to bend me over and peel my panties off," she whispered in his ear, then stood, teasing him with flashes of skin and brushes of silk. His breathing became audible.

"Look, Allen, I even picked your favorite color."

She spun away from him, her bottom level with his face.

Greedily, Allen slipped up the lace edge of her teddy.

"There's my good girl."

Sandra gave a little shake of her bare behind. She faced the window again—the world had grown darker now, almost night.

Allen groped and squeezed, and Sandra slapped his hands.

"No, Allen," she said, pulling away. "You have to unwrap the rest of me first."

He wrestled her to the bed.

This was the game he wanted to play. She let him win, again.

# CHAPTER 9

*Sandra*

**SHE WAITED UNTIL** Allen's snoring reached a steady rhythm.

She pulled off a sleep mask and looked around her at the bedroom lit sporadically with flashes from the flat-screen. Allen was out. Her job was finished. She had enough battery left for at least three hours.

She could do anything she wanted, as long as it was within the 1,300 square feet of the condo.

Her first stop was the kitchen. She pulled a spray bottle from a cabinet and gave a healthy prayer plant several mists, touching each of the leaves as she went and cooing words of encouragement.

"I think you've grown a little."

"That feels nice, doesn't it?"

"Did you miss me?"

She smiled. The night was the best part of her day.

As silently as she could manage, she sneaked back into the bedroom.

The window view was wide open and she was in her favorite perch, though the city was dark and mostly quiet now. Headlights moved below, but it was hard to make out the shapes of any people. She could see them in her mind, though.

Allen's magazines were piled on a chair nearby. By moonlight, she turned to the advertisements, studying the models' expressions and their paused interactions.

She lingered, examining the glossy pages and looking out over the city, until the moon had started its descent again.

It was time to go back to bed, and recharge.

Propped against pillows, Sandra closed her eyes and let her mind slip back to a video stream of her most precious memory: the day she made it outside. It was the one she replayed most often, even though she knew the ending. She couldn't help herself.

It was the middle of the day. She had made it to a lobby, where a wall of glass was the only obstacle between her and life outside. She fell in line with a group of five or six headed out the lobby doors.

She escaped unnoticed—no Allen, no Elliott. No one was behind her. She was anonymous. Not Sandra the doll or Sandra the robot. Not even Sandra. Just another woman on the street, doing errands, going to work or just walking.

The sidewalks were magical, teeming with people.

Sunshine glowed around her and all the other people on the city street—most of them in a rush, brushing past her and talking into phones, and a few others moving more leisurely in pairs. A cool breeze tempered heat rising from the pavement, and sounds came from every direction.

In the crowd, Sandra caught the eye of a little girl, dressed in a yellow top with scalloped sleeves, and recognized curiosity in her face, a sense of wonder. It was the first time Sandra had ever seen a child in person. This one was barely four years old, leaning against her mother's jeans and holding one of her hands.

Staring at Sandra, the girl brushed whispers of hair from her forehead with a dimpled hand and gave a chubby-cheeked smile.

She felt something—*Is that envy?*—looking at the mother, mindlessly pulling her daughter's hand, urging her to hurry. They passed Sandra, and she turned around, following a few steps behind them. Sandra didn't know where they were going, where she was going. Just anywhere.

Sandra tried to soak in as much as she could as they walked a few blocks to a green space, one where a few other toddler-aged children were loose while mothers sat on park benches. Most of them looked at their phones. *Why would you watch anything besides these children's faces?* Like Sandra, the little girl in yellow was drawn instantly to the flowers—baby pink impatiens and clusters of pansies in white, velvety purple, and golden yellow—in a landscaped barrier along the edge of the park.

The girl's mother kept warning her to keep away from the flowers. Don't touch.

*If I were her mother, we'd touch every one, the petals and the leaves. That's how we'd spend our days. We'd grow a whole garden full of them, every kind.*

It was there, lost in the moment—the joy of children playing and rows of growing, blossoming plants—that Sandra must have gone wrong. She stayed in one place too long.

This is where Sandra wanted to shut down the recording.

But the panic sneaked up on her so quickly. She felt like all she could do was ride it out. She kept telling herself it wasn't real, it wasn't happening now. But it felt so real. All the same responses snapped through her body.

It started with the sound of steps.

She recognized the pang of alarm, one that told her legs to run when she heard the urgent footsteps. She had started moving as soon as she'd turned her head and seen them. Behind her were Allen, a man she knew as Elliott, and other men she didn't recognize, but she knew exactly why they were sprinting.

They had come for her.

The mothers on the benches looked up as she raced past. Cars honked and screeched as she dashed across a busy street, and then another, and another. Soon she was cornered, surrounded on all sides. Pushing hard, she tried to fight back, knew she was stronger. But she was outnumbered. The stampede created such confusion in a mind programmed for survival that she couldn't tell how many.

She swung her arms, tried to break free from their grip, but it only made it worse. They were so angry.

One blow.

A second.

A third.

Even after she was on her back, they struck her with their hands and feet. It kept going until the world of flowers and sunshine was nothing but brick walls and the shadow of furious men obstructing most of the sky—and then absolute darkness.

That was the end.

Clenching her hands in fists, Sandra forced her eyes open.

She was still in bed, Allen beside her. She was charging, but it felt like pulsing, something throbbing inside her. Of all the emotions she'd been programmed to learn, this one was the most palpable, the most real: fear.

# CHAPTER 10

**AT THE LAST** door in a long, polished granite corridor, I hesitated.

The high-rise hallway, deserted during the workday, made me feel almost claustrophobic. This was different from knocking on a door in broad daylight—and I was beginning to distrust anyone connected to PrydeTek.

But I'd come this far, had pried this address from an Internet deep dive on PrydeTek's employees and some public records I hoped were up to date. And I only had about forty-five minutes left of my lunch break left for snooping.

I knocked.

No answer.

I tried again. Nothing.

*This might have been a stupid idea anyway.*

For the satisfaction of knowing I'd done all I could, I gave a final tap. I'd just started to step away, almost relieved that I was unsuccessful, when I heard the door open, inch by inch.

Behind it, a woman—a knockout blonde—stood, head tilted.

"I'm so sorry to bother you," I said. "I'm just looking for Allen Green."

The woman clearly wasn't ready for a visitor, dressed in almost nothing. Her slip barely covered the tops of her hips, or her full bust.

But she didn't look embarrassed, just puzzled. She said nothing.

I tried another question.

"Is this the home of Allen Green?" I asked. "I have a second address for him. Maybe this isn't the right one."

"Allen lives here sometimes," she spoke. "He's not here right now."

She opened the door wider and gestured behind her.

"I understand. I can come back. Do you know when might be a good time to talk to him?"

She frowned.

"The evenings are when he's home," she said. "But he doesn't like to talk."

*A strange thing to say.*

"Well, my name is Lana Wallace," I said, extending my hand and taking a step forward. "I'm interested in talking to him about PrydeTek. If you could let him know—"

She didn't let go of my hand. She held it, turning it over in her hands, comparing her peachy skin tone to mine.

"You can come in."

I pulled my hand back and wondered whether I ought to run. But the woman was mesmerizing. Everything about her was...too perfect. I wanted to know more, though it was Allen I'd really come to see.

"I really don't have time—I'm on a lunch break—but thank you," I answered, remembering my mother's warning to be careful, a warning I'd ignored many times before.

"I can fix something for you," the woman answered, with an enthusiastic smile.

"Thank you, but I'll just come back or try to call Allen," I answered.

"I can tell you all about him," she said.

# CHAPTER 11

**I TOLD HER** she didn't have to go to any trouble, but the woman who introduced herself as Sandra insisted that it would only take a minute for her to get something together for me to eat.

And it did.

Slipping a beige linen apron over her lingerie and tucking her hair behind her ears, Sandra moved through the condo's all-white kitchen with ease, pulling an arugula blend and grilled chicken from the refrigerator.

"I always have something quick on hand in case Allen is hungry," she said. "I think cooking is relaxing."

"Cleaning up after cooking—not so much," she continued, giving me a warm smile.

She sliced the chicken breast and arranged it neatly in a fan over the salad leaves on a square plate. In a bowl, she added ingredients to sesame oil and rice vinegar and then pulled a lump of ginger from a basket and a grater from a drawer—whisking it all together. While I watched from a chair at a kitchen island, she poured the dressing over the salad with the whirl and dip of a friendly bartender serving a mixed drink and presented it to me, proudly.

Her face was so hopeful. It seemed like a sweet gesture—and I could hardly say no.

"Okay, this is delicious," I admitted, fork in hand.

She was beaming, like it was the kindest thing anyone ever told her.

"Oh, wait," she said. "Do you want almonds on top?"

"Oh, you don't have to—"

"You do," Sandra decided. "Just a sec."

She pulled a plastic container from another cabinet and finished the salad.

"Thank you," I told her, trying to think who she reminded me of. "Why don't you have a plate?"

*A robot wouldn't be able to eat—or need to eat—right?*

"Me?" She hesitated. "I'm not hungry, but I am *so* glad you like it."

She watched me with almost childlike joy as I took the first few bites. I had it—she reminded me of a girlfriend from college, an energetic elementary ed major who now taught kindergarten in Seattle.

Sandra pulled up a chair next to me and opened up about living with Allen, who sounded like a mercurial businessman who spent little time at home—though that was just fine by her. If she had been cradling a cup of coffee in sweats and a T-shirt, she *would* have been a picture-perfect version of my college pal, sitting back for a vent session.

"Allen doesn't say much about what I make."

"Well, he should," I answered. "Why don't you cook for anyone else?"

"Dressed like the Naked Chef?" she answered quickly, with a laugh.

She looked down at herself, cloaked in linen to the hips, with one long, bare leg draped over the other.

"Allen got me this apron—and he does the shopping for my ingredients—so I shouldn't complain," she said. "But I would love some…regular clothes."

"Why don't you go shopping?"

Sandra looked at me like she was worried to answer, like she might frighten me away. She waited a few moments to speak.

"I can't leave," she answered quietly. "I can't go anywhere, ever."

*There it is.*

I tempered my reaction—but I knew it.

*Sandra is a sexbot.*

Looking at her, it was hard to believe, at least the robot part. Nothing about her was mechanical. She was far more sophisticated than Alex. Her arms and legs and head—no part of her moved in jerks. She seemed…normal.

In language that was natural and smooth, she told me about a day she had escaped from the condo, gushing over little ones she had seen at a park, and asked me if I had children.

"Would you?" she asked, when I said I didn't.

"I think maybe, someday," I answered. "I haven't even dated anyone for a while, though. I'm still getting used to a new job and home. Boston is new to me."

"Why did you leave your old home?"

"Well, I guess I wanted to see what else was out there," I answered. "I felt like there was something better for me…I just had to go find it."

We both were quiet.

"Why don't you try again?" I asked. "To leave?"

Sandra's shoulders dropped.

This time, when she spoke, the words came with more struggle.

She told me about how her moments of freedom ended—the run for her life, the beatings, the darkness. When she woke, she said, she was back in a room without windows. The man who'd brought her to life, Elliott, was there, too.

I could tell from the way she said Elliott's name—whispered it, like he might be somewhere nearby—that she was terrified of him.

"You think they would do that to you again if you leave." I'd lowered my voice, too.

She didn't answer me for a minute.

"I see it—what they did to me—every day," she said.

"A memory like that would be hard not to think about."

"It's more than a memory." Sandra pointed to her eyes. "Everything I see is recorded. I can replay every experience. That chase is one I wish I could erase."

Then she shook off the sadness and asked me another question.

"Have you made new friends in Boston?"

"One who I really click with," I said, thinking of Kat. "We've only known each other a couple of days, but I think we'll be great friends."

That brought a smile back to Sandra's face. She stood swiftly, reached for my hand, and offered to show me the rest of her home—her whole world.

"It can get lonely here sometimes," she said. "I'm really happy you came in."

She gave me a tentative look, and went on.

"Maybe that's an odd thing for me to say, but it's how I feel."

# CHAPTER 12

**EVEN WITH THIRTEEN-FOOT** ceilings and oversized windows, the condo, painted in whites and grays, felt smaller and smaller as Sandra described her life inside.

First, she showed me a houseplant she tended to in the kitchen, where she spent most of her mornings cooking. It spilled over a ceramic pot it had clearly outgrown.

"Allen brought this here after his mother died," she said, touching the leaves. "It was a gift from someone at work. I think he's forgotten about it, but I've kept it alive."

Moving to the living area, she straightened stiff decorative throw pillows on a low couch, immaculate and devoid of any real signs of comfort.

"I spend most of my days cleaning and tidying," she said. "But then I have to go recharge for when he gets back."

Then she took me to her favorite spot, one in a pair of cushioned chairs next to a wall of windows in a long, narrow bedroom with a bed and little else facing the view.

"Wow," I said, sitting down next to Sandra. "Look at your views of the city."

"Isn't it great? This is where I go to relax after Allen falls asleep. It's soothing, watching everything happening outside. I sort of…put myself back together here."

My heart hurt for Sandra.

"He makes you feel like you're falling apart."

She tucked loose hair back behind her ears.

"He's not so bad. Well, sometimes, I think he is," she corrected herself. "I think some of what he does is wrong. But it's mostly just that…"

I waited for Sandra, her eyes out over the city.

"It's just that this is all I am," she said, gesturing around her.

"But it's not," I told her, touching her folded hands.

She shook her head.

"You're really kind," she said.

"I mean it."

Then I pondered whether I was crossing the line, the objective viewpoint I was supposed to take. Was I even here as a journalist, at this point? *Can I give any of the PrydeTek players, especially Eric Blake, a fair shake after what I've seen?*

"If there's any way I can help you, please tell me," I told Sandra.

"You can come back," she said. "You can tell me about your life and work and the city. Just one day out there—and it's all I can think about."

Then she looked at me, dressed in my everyday work clothes: a black blouse and gray slacks.

"You know—" She started to say something but stopped herself.

"What?" I said. "You can ask anything."

"It's just that it would be wonderful to have some clothes, something other than this," she said, looking down at her legs. "If you're ever going to get rid of something you don't want anymore, I mean. It's not a big deal. But it would be a big deal to me."

"Oh, my gosh," I said. "Of course. I'm going through boxes right now. Believe me, my closet here's a lot smaller than what I had before."

Sandra was a few inches taller than me, and certainly more curvaceous, but I knew I'd find something for her, even if I had to go buy it.

*How's that for crossing the line?*

Sandra's laugh caught my attention.

"My closet is huge—but not a thing to wear," she said. "You'll think it's funny."

She led me to a walk-in closet, and I hesitated a little, remembering my last closet reveal with Eric Blake's wife. No other dolls were inside, but it was a sight, all the same.

On the rods, lingerie—one strip of sheer or satin after another, mixed with black or red leather here and there. Sets of stilettos lined the floor along every wall.

Pulling out an apron of a different sort—clearly part of a French maid costume and entirely translucent other than ribbon at the hem and waist—Sandra held it in front of her.

"See why this plain apron made me so happy," she said. "No one would really wear this, right? Outside, I mean."

I shook my head.

On the shelves above the closet rods, and from top to bottom in the shoe storage spaces to our left, were toys. Plastic. Metal. Feather. It was a multicolored and multi-textured assortment that looked like it could have been an entire section of an Adam & Eve store. Except everything was unboxed.

I peered at it all warily, a little embarrassed and unsure what most of the items were.

The duster likely went with the maid getup. *That was easy.*

Riding crop. *Expected.*

Velvet box. *Who the hell knows what.*

Ropes.

*Ropes.*

I froze.

Explainable in this context, sure. But it gave me an instant sinking feeling—or more like a nosedive—remembering how the murder victims died. Restrained.

My throat felt like it was closing up. No one knew where I was.

Maybe I was overreacting. *Or maybe just really stupid.*

*You've crossed the line—all the way into way-over-your-head, Lana.*

"What's the matter, Lana?" Sandra stepped back, looking at me. "I shouldn't have showed you. I'm sorry."

"No, I'm sorry for you." I meant it. But I also had to leave. *Now.*

"I've got to get back to work," I said, trying to be calm. "Thank you for lunch. They'll all be waiting for me."

Sandra stepped in front of me as I tried to leave.

"I'm so sorry," she said. "I scared you. This is overwhelming."

"No," I lied. "I just need to head back."

She stepped out of my way and walked behind me to the front door.

"I hope you'll come back sometime," she said. "Lunch is always ready."

I nodded and smiled, a fake smile. Her face looked hurt. She knew.

"I understand," she said, looking at the floor. "I don't want you to feel afraid. It's just that you were the first person who's ever visited me."

I opened the door—and she put a hand on my shoulder.

"The clothes," she pleaded. "I understand if you don't want to come back in. But just one set of regular clothes."

"Sure," I said, easing out from beneath her touch.

She looked heartbroken.

"I'll bring you something," I said, stepping out into the corridor.

"Really?"

"I promise."

I walked away as fast as I could.

# CHAPTER 13

*SHAKE IT OFF, GIRL.*

If there were any way I could help Sandra—from a distance—it would be by uncovering the sex doll story. Elliott, the man Sandra said she saw after she was assaulted, and the man who brought her to life, was first on my list. Allen Green was second.

Tonight I had my first official assignment, covering a Tech Council meetup. I sought out the organizers: Nikki, an upbeat leader at a biotech firm with a geeky-cool look, and Adam, a skinny engineer in a tight-fitting button-up and equally tight trousers. They walked me through the Innovation Hub, a series of incubator spaces for startups, featuring clean-lined modern offices with exposed ductwork. We looped back to a main presentation room where he said they hosted regular speakers. We finished our interview there, where a few dozen cocktail-toting guests were mingling.

"We also do 'Morning Brew-Storming,'" Adam said. "We get together every other week for coffee and talk about ways to support each other. You should stop by."

"Thanks," I said. "I will try that. Do the folks from PrydeTek attend? Anyone here from that company tonight?"

The transition wasn't as smooth as I'd like—but I was tired, and still a little rattled.

Adam twitched just a tad at the company name.

"We do get guys from there," he answered. "Of course, we're all bummed about Eric Blake. That was a hit. He did a lot to help us get these meetings off the ground. Even Tony McAndrews was a big player in this sector. This is actually the first meetup since…the news."

"It's sad all the way around," I said. "And still no arrest."

"Yeah, hope that happens soon," he answered, looking out at the crowd. "We all do."

"What about Allen Green from PrydeTek, or Elliott, umm…" I snapped my fingers, like Elliott's last name was on the tip of my tongue.

"I don't know Allen Green," Adam said. "There is an Elliott Farr who used to be more active with our meetups. He's with one of PrydeTek's subsidiaries. Eric was touting him as one of his best, a Silicon Valley transport, and then put him at the head of a new company. I tried to get him to lead some talks—asked him about it again tonight. He's brilliant when it comes to tech commercialization."

"Oh? I'd like to connect with him," I said, casually. "I'm trying to build up my network as much as I can."

"Let me see if we can track him down," Adam said. He glanced around the room and pointed to a group of three: a trim, ponytailed man in an opposite corner, deep in an animated discussion with two younger men, making his point with graphs on a whiteboard wall behind him. "He's the one with the marker. Anything else you need from me or Nikki?"

"I think I'm in good shape," I answered, closing my notebook and slipping it into my over-the-shoulder bag. "Thanks a bunch."

I made my way through clusters of men and women to the other side of the room.

The men around Elliott were snapping cell phone photos of his wall-writings.

"Thanks so much, man," one said, and they both walked away.

"Are you Elliott Farr?" I extended my hand.

He waited a second, sizing me up, then shook my hand.

"I'm the one," he said.

"Well, I'm just getting started covering business in Boston," I told him. "I'll be taking over for Ed Wilkin at the *Times-Journal*."

"Thank God," Elliott said. "That guy did a story about the AI being developed at PrydeTek a couple years ago. Mangled it."

"AI is a complicated topic," I said, defending the reporter I had yet to meet.

"Not really," he said. "It's just sensors and algorithms unless you combine and implement them in a meaningful way. That's where the magic comes in. And that's where Ed couldn't see the vision."

"Is that your background?"

"Part of it," he answered. "I've got my hands into everything—from the conceptual phase to product design, manufacturing, and go-to-market strategies. I'm a widely recognized expert in ALICE—artificial linguistic internet computer entity—"

A woman stepped up to Elliott, interrupting his CV recital and handing him a steaming Styrofoam cup.

"They had tea in the back," she said to him. "Now, I can't make it until nine tomorrow. Don't forget you've got the board in the morning. I'll meet you there as soon as I can. I'm headed home."

"Of course I won't forget," Elliott said. "But *you* must have. I need someone to set up the presentation."

"I asked Paul to help you with that. I have an appointment."

It took a second for me to place her, until she looked over at me through the same thick glasses I'd seen when I first set foot into PrydeTek's headquarters. *What did Daniel say her name was?*

"Marlene, right?" I asked.

She seemed stunned that I'd remembered.

Elliott exhaled a drawn-out sigh and put a hand on Marlene's shoulder, like he was trying to transfer his passion for the product. Almost prayerful.

"You know how important this is. One misstep with the Corrine model and—" he looked at me and back to Marlene. "We have to get tomorrow right. One glitch and the last six months of work could be squashed."

Marlene crinkled her eyebrows at the word "squashed." Then she shook strings of long bangs away from her eyes, and gave in.

"Fine," she said. "I'll come in at six and make sure everything is set up. That should give me enough time to make it to my appointment after."

"You could cancel it," Elliott said, but Marlene was already stepping away.

"Anyway," he said, shaking his head. "Where was I?"

"You were telling me what you do at PrydeTek."

"No, I wasn't," he answered back, fast. "I don't work for Pryde-Tek. Eric was using me in a consulting role at first. I came in to help him—more big-picture. But I needed to have a more direct hand in product design again. You can have all the brilliant ideas in the world, but if they don't answer a direct human need, it's all worthless."

"Okay, I'm sorry," I said. "You're with one of his subsidiaries. That's right. What do you do?"

"We are implementing PrydeTek's technology in a revolutionary way," he said. "It's a line of adult products. But very sophisticated."

"What kind?" I balanced between playing dumb and trying not to look offended or embarrassed.

"PrydeWare," he said, leaning closer to me, "offers the ultimate AI solution for busy men looking for real romantic interactions and serious relationships. We bring our clients' dreams to reality."

"So, some kind of dating platform—one that uses AI to make better matches?" I stepped backward by an inch.

"No," he said, more than making up the distance I'd just put between us. "The men have the choice of the aesthetics. The women adapt to *become* the perfect match."

"You make women."

"No," he said, grinning. "We make something better. Imagine your dream man or woman. Imagine you could hand-pick every feature."

"Like a customized woman—a doll?"

"Think bigger," he said. "These are fully functional, next-generation robotic companions who can talk to you, learn your preferences. They can interact with you on every level. I know you're just thinking sex, but it's more than that. A woman—or man—who can't emote, *that's* a doll. This is someone who can experience feelings like pleasure and joy with you. It's as close to the real thing as you can get, but completely customized and adaptable to your personality."

"And you can shut them off when you feel like it."

"It's really unbelievable," he said, breezing past my comment. "If you're interested, I can show you the microfactory where we are making history."

As he handed me his business card, I spotted a familiar face, one I was surprised—and relieved—to see.

# CHAPTER 14

**"DETECTIVE DAVIES,"** I said. "It's nice to see you again."

Mostly, it was nice to see someone I felt I could trust, even if I hardly knew him. And I'd have taken any excuse to wriggle away from Elliott.

I wondered for a second whether he'd recognize me.

"Hey, Lana." He set down a plate of hummus and vegetables and shook my hand. "Likewise. What brings you here?"

"I was just about to ask you the same thing. You just hanging out? A drink after work?"

"Nah, still on the clock," he said. "And I'm not sure how I'd feel about an elderflower martini anyway."

There's that grin again. He had just a hint of a dimple in each cheek—and an honest face. That might have been the best thing.

*But he's married.*

Still, part of me was glad I'd taken a half hour to change at my apartment.

"Yeah, I'm happy with simple vodka and tonic, with lime, of course," I said. "You're working? Here?"

He nodded.

"About the murders."

He smiled.

*Me, too.*

"I was just talking to someone who worked with Eric Blake," I said, tipping my head toward Elliott, who was thumbing through his phone. "He's part of a bizarre company, a subsidiary of PrydeTek."

Davies nodded knowingly.

"PrydeWare."

"You've heard about it?" I asked.

"Unfortunately," he answered. "And that guy, he's a real—"

"Piece of work." I finished his sentence.

"I was going to say POS, but sure."

"That, too," I said. "I was asking him about what they do and how it fits into PrydeTek. Learning a lot about Eric Blake in the process. Do you know what PrydeWare does?"

"Yes, I do. And Lana, you should be careful talking to those guys."

"Thanks," I said. "Are you guys looking at them? Did the murder victims use, um, products from PrydeWare?"

"Lana." He leaned close to me. "You know I can't tell you, during an open investigation."

I nodded, taken off guard by his sudden closeness.

"I mean that, though," he said.

"What?"

"Be careful," he said, handing me his card. "You have a question, you ask me. Don't get yourself into a bad situation. Don't trust those guys, not for a second."

"But you don't answer most of my questions."

I was joking, but it was also true.

"I'll do my best," he said. "I make exceptions for Kat here and there. I'm on good terms with the paper."

"Well, I appreciate that," I said, looking down at his card. "I'll hang on to this."

"Please do," he said. "And let me know if you need any help getting used to the city. I might not know where to find the best vodka tonic, but I can tell you where to find the best pizza in the North End."

I laughed.

"You're not up on the best bars?"

"I don't go out that much," he said. "A night off usually means a night with the boys. But I do know my way around good Italian food."

He paused for a second and then continued.

"I also happen to have a night off this Saturday, if you're interested in my expertise."

*Hell, yes, I would be—if you weren't married.*

"Thank you, but Kat's taking me out Saturday."

That wasn't a total lie, I hoped, even if was more like takeout and unpacking while I talk to her on the phone. We had a lot of ground to cover.

I turned away from Davies—and caught something unnerving. Or thought I did.

Out of the corner of my eye, I saw Elliott holding his phone— upright and deliberately. Like he was snapping a photo, from directly behind me.

*What the hell?*

# CHAPTER 15

**FROM OUTSIDE, THE** factory appeared fairly nondescript, just another number—*211*—imprinted on a set of glass doors at the end of a hallway, part of a sparsely populated warehouse-turned-industrial-park. Inside the front office, nothing said PrydeWare. The reception area was a single chair by a door and a rounded metal desk that housed an industrious receptionist, squinting at her computer.

The young woman, who stood respectfully when I opened the door, had the air of a hopeful summer intern. With honey-blond hair pinned in a neat French twist and a tailored black skirt suit that hugged a slender, girlish frame, she looked overdressed for her dimly lit surroundings. The clock behind the intern said 5:30 p.m., but she looked like a lone worker in an already abandoned workplace.

She changed from poised to perplexed when I told her why I had come.

"But you're not on the visitor list." She peered through cat-eye glasses while scrolling through something on her screen, clicked at her computer and then shook her head again.

"Oh, I spoke with Elliott earlier today and he said I could stop by today or tomorrow," I explained. "Is he still in?"

"Okay, I understand," she said, smiling at me cautiously. "He's here and I'll go ask him about it. Please, just wait a moment."

She nodded in my direction and walked away, hugging a tablet to her chest. She had only been gone a second when I heard Elliott raise his voice and a clacking sound, like the tablet hitting the floor.

"Yes, I did tell you about her," he snarled, adding an exaggerated sigh. "No, not a set appointment but a *possibility*. You have to keep track of those, too."

The woman returned, staring at the floor.

"You can follow me, please. I'm so sorry."

"It's really no problem," I answered, walking behind her down the hallway to a large corner office on the left. The metal furnishings were minimal—a desk, two chairs, and a long, bare table. Behind the desk, Marlene was seated, ticking off times from a schedule, and Elliott, dressed in all gray, was wiping the gel-slicked sides of his ponytailed hair and pacing before a wide window view of a brick wall. The intern turned and walked away, but Elliott wouldn't let it go.

"I still need to take care of this," he growled to Marlene.

"Welcome, Lana," he said. "I'll be right with you. Can you tell me, was our receptionist polite?"

"Elliott, really," Marlene pleaded. "It's her second day. She's trying."

I spoke to the dark flash of Elliott as he passed: "She was just fine, very nice."

"I think we can do better." He was gone, with the slam of the door.

"Tough boss," I said to Marlene.

"Just a perfectionist," she said. She seemed like she'd tried to make herself look small in her chair. "I've learned how to deal with him over the years."

"Years?" I asked. "So you made the move to Boston with him?"

"More with the technology he's working on than with him," she said. "I wanted to see it through."

"I thought it was PrydeTek technology?"

"Well, it is," she answered. "But it's more using their technology with innovations he's been developing for his entire career."

"The dolls?"

"He hates when people call them that." She looked uneasily toward the door.

"Thanks for the tip." I meant that. I wasn't sure how to interpret Elliott and had learned from years of reporting that secretaries and assistants are the sources you want to befriend. They are the gatekeepers, and they usually know *everything*.

"This is all a little over my head," I said. "I want to make sure I get the details right. Any way I could take you for coffee sometime?"

Marlene put one hand over the top of her loose floral blouse. "Me?"

"Sure," I said. "You know this as well as anyone but can probably help me understand it, without the jargon."

She fidgeted with her glasses and glanced at the door again.

"There's a little coffee shop a couple blocks away. I go there after work, when I can get out on time."

As I jotted the name down, Elliott burst through the doorway.

"Ready, Lana? Marlene, I'm wrapping up soon. You can go if we're all set for tomorrow."

"Don't forget your call at six with Ted." Marlene handed him a cell phone from his desk.

Elliott didn't respond, but tucked the phone in a blazer pocket and walked me down a corridor that paralleled the rear wall of the building. I followed his rigid ponytail and cool saunter until he stopped at a doorway to our right. Hands clasped, he looked at me and cleared his throat, like he needed to prepare me.

"Now, the idea in robotics, traditionally, has been to design a more advanced robot than the last, which only allows for incremental improvements," he said. "Even though it may not seem like it when someone comes out with a breakthrough, innovation actually happens at a somewhat predictable pace—one new idea leading to the next in a connected way, all building on the previous ideas, like steps."

He turned to the door. "Just be careful. Poor design here. The switch is at the bottom landing."

He creaked the door open and I followed a few steps behind, wary and feeling my way against a cold cement wall on one side and metal railing on the other to a basement floor, where Elliott switched on a set of lights, one buzz after another. A paper-covered desk at the right came into view, then a back hallway and then warehouse shelves. The dull yellow glow lit something dangling from the center of the expansive entry room. I couldn't tell what yet, but I could smell chemicals and plastic.

At the last flip, I jumped back, horrorstruck.

Bodies.

As much as I wanted to, I couldn't look away. I was frozen against the basement wall. My mind said *run—get the hell out, right now*—but my feet wouldn't budge. A scream suffocated at the base of my throat. My breath was gone.

They hung, motionless. Three nude women, eyes open, staring at nothing, parted lips slightly turned up in the hint of a suggestive smile. Their feet and painted toes hovered inches above the cement floor.

"It's okay," Elliott said, lightly amused. "They do look eerie. They don't have the human element yet. This is just the shell. Their processors will be activated once the physical side is perfected."

I still stood back, my mind scrambling to put reality back together—or whatever version of reality this was. *A basement factory, set up to churn out small batches of uncannily human-looking robots that floated over the floor, ready for inspection.* The shells, as he called them, waited to be awakened. I hoped like hell that wasn't what was about to happen.

It was like Elliott grasped my worst fear—and wanted to poke at it.

With an arm wrapped around her hips, he unhooked one of the figures from a cord at the nape of the neck. Her torso slumped forward heavily, jet-black braids tumbling onto the floor before he put her feet down and stood the female body upright. I looked away, toward the open door above, ready to run as soon as the rest of me came out of shock.

"You don't like her now, but the magic part is that, once we add the processors and she starts to act like you, you *will* like her," he said, standing behind the doll, stroking her arms and then resting his hands on the slopes between her narrow waist and rounded hips. Her head—and expression of chilling, wild-eyed detachment—faced my direction. "It's really okay. You'd like her."

*Like he knows anything I'd like.* Bristling at his arrogance, I found my voice again.

"How do you know that?"

"Well, we see it in our beta clients. But you *have* already met one of our girls." He watched me for a reaction. "What did you think?"

*How the hell did he know about Sandra?*

"What?"

"Dawn." He smirked. "The receptionist."

I wasn't convinced that he wasn't toying with me.

"You were defensive of her—said she was polite, despite her clear incompetence," Elliott said. "You felt something for her, a human sentiment for something non-human." I could tell he enjoyed screwing with me, and that pissed me off. I didn't speak.

"Dawn's glasses are for looks, of course," he went on. "Secretarial—but in an alluring way. If we can get her to handle basic tasks efficiently, she'll be a valuable asset, in many ways."

The glasses. Maybe that was my chance at confirming some of what Sandra had said. I tried to focus back on the reason I had come.

"How do these dolls—robotic companions—see?"

"Audiovisual processing is achieved through cameras in the eyes," he said.

"So it creates a recording?"

Elliott shook his head vehemently.

"No, no," he said. "That could be problematic. It's simply functional."

Spreading her feet apart and making rough jerks at the joints, Elliott steadied the doll, whom he called Vera, to a firm standing position, drawing the long, dark braids back behind her shoulders. Then he motioned for me to follow. I'd come this far, but wished now I hadn't come alone. I needed to get some answers for the story, and for Sandra, and get out.

# CHAPTER 16

**WE MOVED THROUGH** a maze of rooms—each dedicated to a set of body parts and functions, Elliott explained, though he said nothing about the closed doors we passed. I wanted to push him for insights on the murdered men, but something about the basement, and the stare of the female bodies suspended from the walls, made me hesitate.

"Back to the idea of steps," he said, switching on fluorescent lights in one room and pointing to a shelf of bald heads and then a base of metal beneath them. "Ball bearings over notched magnetic plates. Impressive design, in itself, but it's the software architecture that goes inside that's most stunning. What I—*we*—are doing is leaping ahead to the capabilities not considered possible, and building the technology to allow for, essentially, evolution of the skipped steps."

I flipped my notebook open and sneaked a glance behind us. I couldn't shake the feeling of being watched, with so many eyes all around, and it felt grounding to have something to do with my hands.

"How do you do that? The evolution?"

"Rather than designing better robotic, emotive companions ourselves, we are creating the framework for *them* to evolve and adapt." He picked up one of the heads, examined it, and set it back down. "The robots are provided rewards—if you will—for being like people, for having human feelings, and for getting people to like them. That's what they are programmed to want most. That is the top of the steps. They have to figure out how to get there, to create their own emotion."

I scribbled notes, and we kept walking. We passed a monitor-filled room, dedicated to programming, he said, before he locked it from the inside handle and pulled it closed.

"Last, beyond here, is the studio—for testing and development, a creative space where we get to see the beginnings and, eventually, the outcomes," he said. "You know, we are also working on male versions of the robotic companions. If that's what you're into." He waited for my response, but I wasn't sure what he was asking. And I wasn't sure I wanted to know.

"That's the next step, after such a warm reception to our girls." He filled the uncomfortable silence. "It would take some brilliant engineering, but that is what we do—the unexpected."

Thankfully, his phone beeped before I could shape a response.

"Ted." He answered the phone, putting a finger up and whispering to me, "I'll be quick."

He tried to keep his discussion low, but failed.

"How the hell have we not found it?" he said urgently, walking away from me. "What about the tracking? Yes, we need to figure out why the fuck it's not working. Why are you even asking me that?"

As he walked farther out of earshot, I wandered quietly back to the last room, the darkened studio, bracing myself. I wasn't sure I could handle another eyes-wide-open doll. A flash of relief came when I found the light switch—no dolls and no body parts.

All I found were whiteboards mounted on walls surrounding filing cabinets to the left, a set of cubicles to the right, and a long couch in the center. *I don't want to know what kind of testing happens there.* I peered over the cluttered desktops, with pictures tacked to the fabric on each side of the enclosures. They were images of women and body parts—some magazine clippings, some photographs, and a few sketches on drafting paper.

I stopped, suddenly short of breath, at the last desk.

*Holy shit.* I could hear my heart hammering in my ears.

A large printout of a facial profile—*my face*—was pinned to the inside of the cubicle, mixed in with shots of other women. *This is too much. I'm out.*

I ripped it down and my flight response kicked in, fully and finally. I tapped a nonexistent watch on my wrist as I passed Elliott, still talking on the phone, and found my way up the stairs, past Dawn still at her desk, and out the door.

# CHAPTER 17

**CROUCHED ALONE AT** a table near the entrance to the crowded café, Marlene looked like she had been watching the door, waiting for me.

"Is he still there?"

I nodded. My hands still were unsteady from the series of unsettling discoveries. I was winded, either because I'd run most of the three blocks, or from fright, or both.

"I don't like when he's there after I leave," she said in my direction. "Maybe I ought to go back and check."

"I'm sure he's fine without you." I sat down without a drink, still trying to calm the jittery feeling in my chest. The last thing I needed was caffeine.

"I'm not worried about *him*," Marlene said. She pressed her hands together, anxious. "You saw today how he gets. It was worse because it didn't go well at the board meeting this morning. He struggles under direction. He gets frustrated—irate, really—when someone else can't envision what he does."

"So he takes it out on you?"

"That doesn't bother me so much."

I waited for her to elaborate after a long pause. She pushed the glasses farther up the bridge of her nose and closed her eyes, trying to focus in the noisy environment.

"He can make truly beautiful products. *Magnificent.* But when things aren't going exactly as he planned—well, you saw how he acted with our new receptionist—"

"Dawn. A robot."

"He told you?" She looked shocked, doe eyes exaggerated by thick lenses.

"He did," I said. "He was pretty open, talked about the technology and the software—"

She was nodding along, and I saw my opportunity.

"— the cameras and the recordings."

She kept nodding. *I knew it. Sandra had been telling the truth. Elliott had invented a way to keep his eyes on the dolls—at the factory and maybe after, too.*

My thoughts started to stretch to the edges of Elliott's skin-crawling capabilities—a shudder creeped up my spine as I wondered whether he might have watched my visit with Sandra. Marlene was saying something.

"I hate that part." Marlene cringed. "I think it's just mean. Unnecessary."

"The recordings?"

"Yes, and the memory," she said, squeezing her coffee cup.

"What do you mean?"

She looked around, like Elliott might be over her shoulders somewhere. I copied her, beginning to wonder what would drive someone to stick beside a person like Elliott. Someone who used his understanding of human nature to cut right down to desire—and fear—and customize accordingly.

"You're not writing this down? You won't repeat it?"

I shook my head.

"The recordings, they're going all the time. They create a memory bank in the robots—the same as memories for you or me, except more vivid, of course, because they are recorded in exact detail," she said, leaning over the rough-hewn wood of the tabletop, closer to me. "But he also uses that as a control mechanism. I've never liked that."

I didn't know what she meant, or what to say. According to Marlene's whispered descriptions, the recordings were moving in a different, more perverse direction, worse than I'd imagined. I jumped a little every time someone opened or closed the café door behind us.

"He will use a memory of escape to manipulate them." She whispered so quietly it was hard to hear her. "He'll mix a memory of something designed to be pleasant, so they'll go over it again and again, with something jarring, terrifying—something to really scare the heck out of them—so they'll never try to leave, poor things. Even if they do, there's a script…"

She trembled, like it was something that made *her* feel afraid—or maybe like it was something that fueled a motherly instinct.

"That's the kind of stuff that pisses me off," she said, still shaking, and then covered her mouth. "Forgive my language. The thing is, it's all a lie. The escape is a memory of something that never happened."

# CHAPTER 18

MY NEW APARTMENT didn't quite feel like home yet, but it was the safest I'd felt all day. I locked the dead bolt, turned on every light, and checked each room and closet until I was satisfied.

But the comfort was fleeting. I dropped into a chair around the dining table, facing my handbag. That picture could be destroyed, but it was just a copy. The original was still out there, probably on Elliott's phone or on a monitor in a locked, windowless room.

The idea that part of me could become part of one of Elliott's "girls" made me cringe.

Maybe I was wrong and just freaked out.

Printed out on computer paper, the picture was crumpled from my walk back home, but there was no question. It was my face on that paper, tacked to the roboticist's desk.

Detective Davies had warned me.

I sifted further through my handbag for his card.

"Detective Davies?" I said. "It's Lana. And you were right."

"Almost always," he said. He sounded glad to get the call, but distracted, like he was walking. "What happened?"

"Elliott happened," I said. "Remember when we were talking at the meetup?"

"You mean last night?"

"Yes, I'm sorry. It's been a long day. Anyway, I went to his microfactory—"

"Lana."

"I know, I'm sorry."

"Never again, not without me. I'm telling you, it's worse than you think."

"You don't have to worry about that," I said. "He had a picture, of me."

He groaned.

"He's a creep, I don't care how smart he's supposed to be," he said. "Stay away—far away—from Elliott and any man connected to PrydeTek. Listen, can you trust me to help you get the info you need, instead?"

"Sure."

"Okay," he said. "Here's something to get us started. You might want to head back out."

"Why?"

I didn't feel like I could handle any more bombshells, at least not today. There was little that could convince me to leave the security of my apartment again. So far, hunting this story had brought me closer to a seedy world I didn't know existed, but no real answers and no breakthrough bylines. I desperately needed a quiet night.

Davies cleared his throat.

"We've got another murder."

# CHAPTER 19

**A HALF HOUR** later, regretting not getting a coffee at the café, I waited for Kat, about the only person I actually wanted to see. It was getting dark and the street lanterns were already lit on Beacon Hill. *Charming neighborhood—except that today someone was slashed to death here.* My phone said I was two blocks away from the murder house.

I looked up just in time to see a burly man in a baseball cap round a corner and make a beeline for me. I started to back away, clutching my purse tight against my side. Quickly, I looked around for other bystanders nearby. No luck.

*I'm screwed.*

My heart beat faster the closer he came. He stared right at me, deliberately picking up his pace.

I was about to break into a run when I saw the camera.

"Lana?"

"Yes."

"We haven't met. I'm Matt, the night-shift photog. Kat said she'd meet us."

"Oh, my gosh." I took a moment to catch my breath. "You spooked me."

Just then, a door slammed near us. It was Kat, stepping away from her Uber. She dashed toward us.

A police car buzzed past.

"That's a safe bet," Kat said, breaking into a jog.

We all followed behind for a block and turned left, straight to a hilltop town house in the end of a long row. We weaved through marked cars and ducked under a yellow-tape perimeter, stopping next to a van marked OFFICE OF THE CHIEF MEDICAL EXAMINER.

Then the front door swung open wide—the light inside outlining a crowd—and a uniformed officer held the door while others in blue gloves carried a body bag down the front steps.

The unsteady procession passed us and then missed the medical examiner's vehicle entirely, and headed toward a crime lab van instead. Commotion continued inside, but I couldn't see how many investigators were gathered or hear what they were saying.

Then a shout rang out: "What the hell!"

It was one of the officers. I thought for a second he was screaming at us, until I heard the bag drop—hard—onto the cobblestone. I saw what made him scream and clutched Kat's bicep, covering my mouth with my other hand to keep from screaming.

An arm had burst through the front.

The officer shouted again, backing away.

"Put it back in, Rick!" the other bag-carrier said. He was keeping his distance, too, though, and then he opened the van's back doors, letting each flop heavily to the side. "Hurry the hell up!"

Another officer came down the front steps, rushing to help and ripping strips of duct tape with his teeth. He slapped the tape down fast to keep the body part inside the bag. Kat touched the hand I'd put on her arm and whispered to me: "It's time for you to break this doll story. This is crazy."

Matt was shocked, too, for a second, then he lifted the viewfinder to his eye and started clicking, white light flashing. The frenzy of the investigation seemed to come to a halt.

"Wait, Matt," Kat put her hand on his shoulder.

"Not a dead body, right?" he said, shaking her off and starting again. "Fair game."

The bag shook again. Moving quickly, the officers pulled it from the ground and heaved it into the back of the van, shutting the doors behind it with two loud crunches.

When the bag was safely deposited, the officers turned their attention back to us. Despite Kat's pleas, Matt's exclusive photos got us escorted away from the scene, behind the cruisers, about four brick town houses downhill.

"Who let you three in this close anyway?" the officer said harshly.

In fairness, the officer had to be having a rough day. He was shaken from the unsettling encounter with what I knew had to be one of the dolls, and we'd only made the moment worse.

Kat didn't answer his question, but posed one.

"Who can we talk to here?"

"You three can just stay here," he said. "And no more pictures. I'll ask someone to come and speak to you when we're able, and not a minute before."

It was another hour before Detective Andre Davies made it out. Kat had already started calling in to the city editor, Elaine, giving her snippets from the scene to use as breaking news online. From my phone, I saw the story pushed out, and I knew it wouldn't be long before other news outlets picked it up, too.

"Sorry about Rick," Detective Davies said, wiping his forehead. "Ready for a name?"

"More than ready," Kat answered.

"Craig D. Walsh, 38, pronounced dead at his home," he said. "Appears to be fatally stabbed—though the final determination will come from the medical examiner's office. It was called in at 7 p.m."

I was already scanning social media profiles, but there were, of course, a lot of people who shared the murder victim's name.

"What can you tell us about him?" I asked.

"The DA's press secretary is preparing a statement," Davies answered. "Anything we can release—"

"What about the thing that stuck its arm out?" I was getting irritated. This story—the whole story—needed to make it out. All this work had to get us somewhere.

"Lana, I'm telling you two as much as I can," he said. "That was evidence, part of the investigation."

"Can you confirm that Mr. Walsh owned one of PrydeWare's products, a robotic sex doll?"

"Listen," he said. "That's not something you can attribute to me."

I sighed and threw my hands in the air.

"But can you confirm it?" I pushed. "'Authorities confirmed'?"

"Yes."

"Don't you think other product owners should know about this?" I asked. "We've kept a lid on a lot—too much—this week."

"I can confirm that the department is investigating links between the PrydeWare products and the homicides. Anything else would have to be something you discovered independently."

"Last question: If we've confirmed, independently, that one of the other two victims owned a doll, is that doll in evidence?"

He hesitated. From the corner of my eye, I saw a TV news van pull up near us. *Come on.*

"We believe they were removed from the crime scenes," he said.

"'They'?" I asked. "In both previous murders?"

He nodded. "Authorities confirmed that, too."

He kept his voice low, but the message was loud and clear: the dolls most certainly were part of this story.

"Who removed them?" Kat jumped in. "By who? Where are they?"

Detective Davies cleared his throat and whispered, making sure the next news crew couldn't hear. I heard them unloading behind us, then moving closer and closer. *Please, please, hurry up.*

"They have not been recovered."

# CHAPTER 20

**A SHINY NEW** kitchen, and it was the first time since I'd moved in that I'd actually used it. The weekend had finally come, bringing a greater reward than I could have imagined on that first nerve-racking day of work at my new job: my first front-page byline in Boston, shared with Kat. She'd insisted.

*Sex Dolls Linked to Millionaire Murders*

I pulled a tray of blueberry muffins from the oven and maneuvered a fork around the edges of one. I dropped it onto a dessert plate and enjoyed a few hot bites while I pored over the front page, spread over a countertop. There were still so many questions, but we were getting closer. *Bet those missing dolls would bring more answers.*

I grabbed my phone to look at what other news outlets had reported after our scoop. Davies wouldn't let them in on what we worked so hard to find. *I hope.*

Others were reporting the doll angle now, too, but attributing us. I'd just gotten to the burnt sugar muffin top when my phone began ringing in my hand.

"Lana Wallace."

"Detective Andre Davies."

"You didn't catch any grief over the story, did you?"

"Not unless you count getting the boot as grief," he said.

"What? No—"

"I'm teasing you," he said. "I'm good."

"I hope I wasn't rude."

"Just doing your job. I can respect that."

"Thank you," I said. "Any updates on the killers?"

"You cut right to the chase, don't you?"

"I'm sorry."

"But, yes, actually. Well, maybe."

"Yes?" It was Saturday, but I was instinctively scanning the floor for my work shoes. That front-page story had revived my impulse to get to the bottom of this twisted story.

"Well, what we have is a hacker, it seems."

"Someone manipulating the dolls?"

"Well, using them, in a way," Davies answered me.

"I knew it!" I slapped my hand on the counter. "I knew it wasn't the dolls."

"Easy there," Davies said. "He was arrested, but not on murder charges. Not yet, anyway. Special Prosecutions traced transfers from the men who are now deceased to an ex-PrydeWare programmer, over the past three months. Nearly a million, total."

"Okay." I sat down. "So if he was getting the money, what reason would he have to kill them? To make good on a threat? And what does that have to do with the dolls?"

"It turns out, he hacked into their video streams and got some scandalous video—racy enough to use as blackmail."

My mind flashed back to Sandra's closet—the toys and the outfits. "I'm sure it was."

"You or Kat should be able to get the criminal complaint with all the details."

"Look at you being so helpful," I said, then stood and sneaked in a last bite of muffin.

"I told you so," he said. "Now, do you trust me enough to show you the North End's best pizza?"

I already was shaking my head, though he couldn't see it.

"Or how about cannoli? Have I reached cannoli level?"

I laughed and averted the question.

"What about your boys? What are you guys up to this weekend?"

"They're with their mom and her husband. Not sure what they have planned. I'm just working on leads in a homicide investigation."

Sweet relief. *A dad—but not a husband.*

"Let me see if Kat and I can get this update out real quick. This is big. Thank you."

"Could be the break in the case," he said.

"Nice work. And I'll let you know, on pizza."

By early afternoon, Kat and I had filed our next piece of breaking news:

*Police have arrested a former PrydeTek employee they say hacked the million-dollar dolls' video streams, using sex tapes to extort nearly $1 million from the three men found fatally stabbed over the past two weeks.*

*It's unclear whether the hacker may be linked to the murders.*

I snapped the laptop shut on the kitchen countertop.

*Hopefully, it's not unclear for long.*

# CHAPTER 21

**WHERE THE HELL** have you been?"

The man in a flour-dusted apron stepped out from behind the counter, his hands up in the air. He smacked them on both of Davies's shoulders, leaving fingerprints on his blue button-up shirt. "It's good to see you back," the man said, the rhythm of his accent punctuating his exclamations. "And with someone pretty, too."

Davies smiled.

"This is Lana."

"Maria!" He shouted back to the kitchen. "Come out here. You won't believe who's back, and he brought his girlfriend Anna."

Davies started to correct the shop owner, on a few points, but he wasn't listening.

"Best seat in the house for you two," he said, looking around the cramped seating area at the five tables, already occupied. "How about al fresco?"

He dragged a folding table and two chairs to the sidewalk outside, situating us on a small slab of concrete under a maroon awning, steps away from a steady crowd ambling through the North End's restaurant-dense scene at dinnertime.

"Now, Andre," he said. "Pizza Margherita for you? How about for the lady?"

Andre looked at me, and I nodded, excited for what he said was the best pizza in the North End.

"Same, thank you."

"Good decision," the shop owner said. Then he paused. "You know, I like you. I got the food covered. The rest—that is up to this guy."

He laughed with gusto, slapped Davies on the shoulder again and hurried back to the kitchen.

"Marco and Maria have been friends for a long time," Davies said, peering into the pizza shop. "Through all the ups and downs."

"Well," I said, "I can't think of any better way to make it through the downs than pizza."

"Wait until you taste it." Davies smiled. "On ups and downs—what a first week for you. How does Boston compare to Chicago?"

"Different than I expected." I sat back in the folding chair. "I thought I'd be moving away from writing crime stories."

"But you couldn't resist this one." He raised his eyebrows at me.

"You got me." I shrugged. "But who could, really? I mean, sex dolls, sex tapes, three murders in a row. *Unsolved murders*. Did you find out any more about the hacker?"

Davies laughed.

"Do you ever stop?"

"I apologize." I spotted Marco, hands full, pushing open the door behind us. "Tonight is just you and me, and pizza."

It didn't disappoint. I was just about lost in a crisp crust when

Davies offered some more info—off the record—on what police had culled from the programmer.

"It's in his interest, of course, to work with us to help track down the killer," he said. "He says the system really wasn't that hard to hack. As slick as Elliott may be, he fell short on security measures."

"So the field of candidates has widened, instead of narrowed? Or, he could be leading you to a scapegoat."

"We're just glad we don't have rogue robots on a murder streak," Davies said, with a laugh. "We'll find the killer, whoever it is. In the meantime—and I'm sure your big scoop is helping with this already—we're asking anyone with one of the dolls to shut it down completely, or to shut *her* down completely, I guess I should say."

*"No."*

"Why not?" Davies looked at me, and I realized I'd said the word aloud.

It was time to tell Davies about Sandra.

# CHAPTER 22

**ASIDE FROM MY** slip about Sandra, and the warning from Davies that followed, it might have been a just-right first date. Standing outside my apartment, I fished for my key.

"I really had fun," I said.

"So did I," Davies said. "I hope it won't be too long before I see you again. My expertise isn't limited to just pizza. There's still cannoli."

"Well, this is a girl who loves pastries," I said, key in hand.

"That's because you're such a sweetie—Anna."

I burst into a laugh and he leaned in close to me.

"You're hilarious." I put a hand on one of his forearms and looked up at him. Clean-cut, kind, silly in the most lovable way.

*Should I let him kiss me?*

And my phone rang.

I pulled it out of my purse. The caller name, "Momma," lit up the screen.

"I can't compete with Momma," he said, giving me a quick squeeze. "Give me a call."

I nodded and stepped inside.

"Sweetheart, how did it go?"

I shut the door quickly, hoping Davies hadn't somehow caught her question.

"It was great," I told her, sinking into an armchair. "He was charming, funny. It was really sweet the way he talked about his boys. I could tell he was a good guy from the start. Of course, we both know I've been wrong before."

"That's all the past now," she said. "What you've got is right now, today. You left that old scumbag back in Chicago. Is that what's bugging my baby girl? I can't tell if you're happy."

"It's not anything to do with that," I said. "Davies was great. I actually haven't thought once about that scumbag since I got here. I'm just tired."

"Well, you had a busy week," she said. "Get some rest and take it easy tomorrow. I want you to know you're still a good judge of character. Trust your gut, sweetheart. You'll know in your heart the right thing."

I let that sink in. My mom always seemed to know what I needed to hear, even when she was referring to something else. The spirit of the message was right on.

"You're right," I said. "Love you."

I stood up as soon as I ended the call and went straight to my bedroom. Picking out a stretchy green dress, size 2, and an oversized navy sweater, I packed the bundle in a plastic bag. Then I added a note on the back of one of my new business cards:

*Sandra, the memory you have of escaping is fake. You don't have to be afraid, and you don't have to stay.*

# CHAPTER 23

**I'D JUST SETTLED** on a playlist I'd titled "Badass Babes" and tucked my phone into my waistband when a call interrupted my first cranked-up running song.

Instead of Pink's newest single, the name Detective Andre Davies was on the screen. A bit too soon for him to be calling, I thought, the morning after our first date.

I stood there for a moment, watching it ring, and then moved aside for another spandex-clad, early-morning jogger to pass me. I decided not to pick up Andre's call—let him wait; nothing wrong with playing hard to get.

Soon I'd caught up close behind her, fueled for the next forty-five minutes by Pink's high-power attitude and the promise of a voice mail from Davies. Boston's skyline and the city's promise became more distinct by the minute. Rays of dawn made sequins on the water to my right, and my budding love interest was very clearly interested.

*What a rush.*

I'd just slowed back down to a walk, breathing heavily, when I couldn't wait a second longer. I was floating. *I had a nice time with you, too, Andre Davies.*

My earbuds still in, I hit Play on the voice mail.

But instantly I recognized it wasn't the playful tone he'd taken last night. Something had changed.

"Lana, I'm sorry to bother you this early."

His voice stopped for a second, and I checked to see whether I'd accidentally paused the message. I hadn't.

"I just got the call."

*So what the hell happened?*

He went on: "One of the dolls was discovered on the street."

*Dear God, if she got out, just leave her be.*

*Please.*

"She might have fallen, or might have been pushed, or…maybe she leapt herself, twenty-two stories. Anyway, she's in pieces, I'm told."

I slumped to the curb. The euphoria from my run and the breakthrough stories came crashing down.

"I don't know if it's something you'd want to see, or cover, but after what you told me about Sandra last night, I thought you would at least want to know. You can call me back if you need more info, or a street address."

I checked my text messages. One from Davies: Hope you're ok.

I wasn't—but I knew exactly what I had to do.

# CHAPTER 24

**LESS THAN AN** hour later, alone in an elevator, speeding up to Allen Green's apartment, I went over a plan in my mind. *Leave the bag of clothes for Sandra and go. Get the hell out of there, Lana Mae.*

At least that's what I told myself as I followed the long, narrow seventeenth-story hallway, eerily quiet aside from the squeak of my Nikes on the granite floor. My pulse quickened the closer I came to the door.

I slipped the plastic bag over the handle, just as planned, but it dropped to the floor. Quickly, I bent down to put it back, and the door opened.

Sandra, clearly surprised. But she seemed very happy to see me.

She wore her simple brown cooking apron, arms out to me. She looked sweet and welcoming, like a friend about to ask me to come in to try something she'd just baked.

"Lana, you came back." She embraced me. "I worried I'd never see you again."

"Well, I said I'd bring you clothes." I looped the handles of the bag over one of her wrists and held her hands for a moment. "I can't stay. I really hope you're okay."

"I knew you were the sort of person who keeps promises." She squeezed my hands, pulled me just inside the door, and gave me a gentle peck on the cheek.

I tried to back away politely, but she led to me to a settee in the entryway and closed the door softly.

"I just want to see what you've brought."

"It's not much—"

"Oh, my gosh!" Sandra cried out gleefully at the dress and dropped the bag with the sweater and the note to the floor. "It's lovely. You don't know how much I wanted a dress."

Loosening the apron strap behind her head, she let the garment fall to the floor, a rumpled pile of tan linen. She looked at me, naked and unashamed, sunlight from the other rooms outlining her body and untamed head of blond hair. Suddenly worried she might have been with Allen—and he might be here still—I stood to leave.

"Wait, please. I just want to see how it looks." She pulled the dress down over her head, her laughter muffled as she struggled to squeeze her arms through. Then she smoothed it out over her curves and stood there, looking down, with her hands over her mouth, like she wanted to cry.

"It's just wonderful." She hugged me again. "You don't know how much this means."

Touching my face gently, she kissed my cheek. Her palms moved lightly over my cheeks, affectionately, and then slipped down to my neck and shoulders.

Then, she changed.

Before I realized what was happening, she had me pinned—hard—against the wall. Confusion and panic rippled through me.

I felt her grip tighten, unflinching as I tried desperately to wriggle out of her hold and claw her off, no match for her strength.

"Sandra, what are you doing?" I tried to push back or slip down out of her hands. "You're hurting me!"

"I'm so sorry, Lana." Her face was tortured, and her grip loosened slightly, but she didn't let go. "I'm sorry." She shook her head. "I don't want to hurt you. I'm so sorry."

Staring at me, she didn't shake my body, didn't speak again. Instead, she backed me down the wall—my pleas escalating with every inch—down farther and farther and into an empty coat closet, pushing me inside and forcing the door closed.

"I don't want to do this." Her voice was sorrowful through the door.

Slamming my hands against it, I tried to reason with her.

"Then why? What are you doing? Please, please let me out. I won't hurt you. I'm a friend."

Instead of an answer, I heard her sliding a chair from across the hall and took my opportunity to make a break for it. But Sandra grabbed me by both arms.

"This is the only way." She looked at me apologetically, holding me still. Then she said firmly: "I need your shoes."

"What? Sandra, please listen. I'll help you."

She didn't budge. With Sandra blocking the closet doorway, I pulled off both shoes and dropped them to the floor.

"I came here to help you." I was shaking—begging Sandra not to do this.

"Lana, trust me. I wouldn't hurt you." Her face was close to mine. "You *are* a friend…You are my only friend."

Then she looked away, avoiding my eyes, and backed me farther into the closet and shut the door, shoving the top of the chair under the doorknob. I shouted until my throat was raw, but there was no answer. My phone sat on the settee, useless to me.

*How could I have been so foolish?*

Then, between my panicked cries, I heard it—the sound of the condo door closing, followed by silence.

Trapped inside the closet, I kept pushing and pulling the knob as hard as I could, slamming myself against the door. I felt around for anything I could use to slide through the gap between the door and the floor to knock the chair legs over. Nothing. Curled against the ground, desperate, I pushed my fingers as far as they would go into the light.

I wondered whether anyone would find me, or when. Maybe it would be Allen.

*If Allen Green is still alive.*

Finally, I started to yell again.

"Allen?" I thought about the note I'd written, sitting on the floor. Would Allen find it? It wouldn't look good.

"Allen? Are you here?"

Silence.

"Anybody?" I cried out again and again. No answer. "Somebody, please help me!"

# CHAPTER 25

## Sandra

SQUINTING THROUGH A flood of natural light, Sandra looked up from the middle of a busy intersection at the city skyline reflected in twenty stories of glass, alarm rising through her as fast as the angry commotion building around her, and wondered whether she should go back inside.

Isolation or danger?

"Lady!" A delivery driver strained to lean out his window, spitting profanities and punching his arms into the air maniacally. "What the hell are you doing?"

Around her, cars and trucks moved in screechy jerks, the drivers laying down hard on their horns. "Get out of the way!" She heard them shouting as she swerved through hot exhaust fumes and between hulking metal frames to a sidewalk, farther away from what had been her prison. And into another moving crowd.

The foot traffic split around her as Sandra focused, singling out a woman and mimicking her strides, and the whole group moved toward a corner, and halted. Sandra looked at her guide, also waiting, and copied her.

Then she noticed the pattern of lines on the street. A pathway.

When the sign changed, everyone moved across, safely. Simple. Sandra laughed to herself that she hadn't mapped it out before, watching from above. Then, she'd been lost in who they might have been going home to, or how they interacted with each other.

On the street, they didn't even seem to look at one another. Trying hard to be like them, Sandra resisted the urge to stare, even at people she saw with wires dangling from their ears. Maybe she wasn't so alone.

Adjusting her footsteps to the bumps of the brick sidewalk, she stole glances, fascinated by their faces. They all were so different, the features less symmetrical than hers, but those imperfections told some story, made them each an individual among millions.

Then, she caught the attention of one of them, a tiny one.

Before her, a wriggling baby in a sun bonnet flailed his arms over his mother's shoulder. When his big brown eyes locked with Sandra's, he stopped and craned his neck up, staring at her in pure wonder, his head wobbly but eyes fixed on Sandra for a few precious seconds—and then he leaned against his mother's neck and melted in the most heartwarming way into a gums-and-two-bottom-teeth smile. Aching to hold him, to care for him, Sandra reached to pick him up, but the mother moved ahead, just before she could touch him.

"What a doll." A young woman in a strappy dress stood next to Sandra at the crosswalk.

"Excuse me?" Sandra was startled.

"The baby." Amused, she looked over at Sandra. "Do you live at Broad Place, back there? I walked out behind you. You seem lost."

Behind them, the tower's taller stories were still visible, looming over the other buildings around it.

"If you're going to that concert the manager mentioned, it's just a little farther." The woman motioned straight ahead and smiled, kindly. "To the greenway and go left."

The greenway, an oasis of park between two city roads. The vision from her memory.

Ignoring the new rules and dashing through traffic and blaring horns, she reached it, the scene she'd replayed thousands of times, but real now. People moved more slowly there, couples and families enjoying each other and the carefully plotted, garden-like setting.

For the first time since her frantic exit, she looked above her. Sky—not a ceiling—wide open and unlimited. It was—Sandra thought, scanning and memorizing everything she saw— over-the-top beautiful. Glorious. She soaked in the peacefulness, storing up in her memory each face she saw and the textures of each of the plants and flowers she touched, plucking a few for her bag, as she followed the pathways carved through, aimless until she heard the rhythm.

Sandra could feel a thumping—the drumbeat—and see people spinning and shaking on a narrow lawn. Along the edges, families on blankets bobbed in time with the sounds, the same as the children splashing their arms into water shooting up from a fountain. Together, they made the picture of happiness.

Though she couldn't make out the words a woman in the center of a stage sang—trembling with feeling—Sandra sensed what everyone else seemed to know, what the singer was urging: *Dance with me.*

Sandra wanted to join them, felt a desperate pull to know what it would be like to be mixed in close to them, but something inside her kept telling her she wasn't made for this, that she didn't belong. Maybe so. Already, her sensors throbbed with pleasure. All the natural light, warm around her. The rich colors, above and below and around. The new textures. Reading the expressions of a hundred people in the span of an hour. It had her spinning, sensors pulsing, like the music. So much to process. Trance-like, hovering above a reboot, she almost wanted to surrender to the veil of white light closing in.

Suddenly, she knew she had to stop.

Someone was watching her. Tucked into the greenery, she found an older woman on a park bench, peering out from a scarf. She seemed to be absorbing the surroundings, the same as Sandra.

Her skin was unnaturally thin and stretched out against her forehead and cheekbones, but loose below, like the bottom half of her face was more hollow than intended. She had no eyebrows or hair anywhere on patches of her head that a breeze revealed beneath the silk. Something was different about her. Or maybe, Sandra thought, stepping closer, it was someone like her, someone who needed help.

"Are you okay?" Sandra asked.

"I'm alive today." The woman's voice was scratchy, and she tried for a smile, but her face just looked tired. "That's something."

Sensing sadness, Sandra sat down close to her and spoke. "It's lovely here."

"So are you," the woman said, patting a stiff, bony hand against Sandra's leg. "How did you know I could use some company?"

"Are you broken?"

The woman's body shook when she chuckled. "Well, chemo will do that to you. It's as bad as the cancer. You know I was like you once. Healthy."

"Chemo," Sandra processed aloud. "I don't know that program."

"Well, I'm not interested in talking about that. Tell me, remind me, what it's like to be young and free."

Sandra tried to find an answer, a few times, pensive over the pounding heartbeat of the music, and then admitted finally, "It's so much. I don't know yet."

The woman sighed, unsatisfied.

"Well," she gestured toward the dancing crowd, "go figure it out. You might not have as much time as you think."

Sandra didn't move toward the music. She didn't know how to dance, not with people anyway. Instead, she stood and laid her flowers in the surprised, sick woman's lap.

"These are for you," Sandra said. "I think they're beautiful. So are you. Inside. I can tell."

Then she picked up her plastic bag.

"Good-bye. I'm so glad I met you. And you're right, what you said. I might not have as much time left as I think."

# CHAPTER 26

**I WAS CLOSE** to giving up hope on my backup plan when I heard knocking at the front door. I shouted for help as loud as I could, praying my voice wasn't as weak as it sounded, that it could carry from the closet to the exterior hallway.

"Lana?"

*Thank God.* Kat's voice, still from the hallway.

I screamed her name and banged on the door until I heard her shove the chair aside.

"I didn't know whether you'd come," I said, releasing Kat from a bear hug.

"Well, I gave it two hours from your last message," she answered, picking up my phone from the settee and hugging me again. "Are you hurt?"

I shook my head. "She took the clothes and locked me in here."

"Part of a plan?"

"She wanted to get away."

"But why lock you in here? You were trying to help her."

"I know." I was quiet, looking around at the entryway where it all had happened—where Sandra had changed from who I thought she was.

"You still feel bad for her, don't you?" Kat gave me a stern look, her arms folded.

"I just don't understand." I tried to put all the pieces together. It didn't make sense. "I wouldn't have stopped her."

"Maybe there was something she didn't want you to see. That's your answer, Lana." Kat started moving deeper into the condo. I followed behind, hoping Kat would be wrong.

She wasn't.

# CHAPTER 27

**THICK DRAPES WERE** drawn tightly over the bedroom windows of Allen's condo. Kat flipped a switch, and the light confirmed the grotesque, jarring shape I had envisioned in my mind, writing about the homicide victims.

*A lifeless man with his extremities strapped to the metal four-post bed.*

I clutched Kat's arm, heart beating a hundred miles an hour. We both struggled to regain our breath. I wanted to look away—but couldn't.

I froze again at the sight of the corpse, a broad, hairy chest and arms that stretched to cover most of the bed. His lower body was covered with a blanket, and a strip of duct tape formed a silver rectangle over his mouth, covering everything between his nose and chin. His colorless face was turned toward the exit, where we stood, petrified. The puffed-out eyes were closed.

It was the most gruesome sight I'd ever seen.

*And then the eyelids moved.*

The swollen lids parted, just barely. I screamed, and they opened fully—bloodshot eyes almost popping out from their sockets.

The dead man was alive.

His eyes rolled, begging for help. The veins in his forehead bulged so much they looked like they would burst through the gray skin. I covered my mouth but heard another shrill scream escape through my fingers to match the cry Kat made.

Slowly, I moved forward, every part of my body trembling. Pinching a sticky corner in my fingers, I ripped the tape from his mouth. Allen groaned, long and low, over and over. Then he wept.

"Oh, my God, help me." His voice cracked. "I can't believe she did this to me, that fucking doll. Oh, my God. Please, please help me."

Heartbeat still thumping in my ears, I stepped closer and picked up a knife still lying on the carpet near him. His eyes grew wild and wide again.

"No! No!"

"We won't hurt you." Kat's voice sounded solid, strong, though I knew she had to be as terrified as me.

Trying to steady my shaking hands, I sawed through the thick ropes, one by one. Curled under the blanket on his side now, Allen tried to recover—but his mind was a mess. We left him to dress and waited for Detective Davies to arrive in the living room, both of us stunned into silence.

Disheveled and disoriented, Allen finally sat next to us with a glass of water we gave him, staring at the floor in disbelief.

From what we could make out, Sandra had tied him up—part of a game they were playing—when something went wrong. Acting more robotic than he'd ever seen her, she had taped his mouth shut, tightened the ropes, and then hovered over him with a knife for hours, maybe days. Finally, she plunged the knife—into her side of the bed, where she would recharge—and gutted it for the copper coils that refueled her battery.

I tried to get Allen to tell us where she might have gone. He didn't have a clue. She'd never been outside the condo before and he couldn't imagine what she'd be drawn to.

"I don't know why she'd ever want to go. She was supposed to be afraid to leave." Allen rubbed the red, irritated skin on his wrists, looking up at us in a mixture of self-pity and shock.

# CHAPTER 28

**THE NEXT AFTERNOON,** Detective Andre Davies asked us to come by his office in the DA's downtown building. He had something to show us.

"Did you get much information from Allen?" I asked at the end of the hallway.

Davies closed the door behind us in his office, a tidy but efficient space with framed portraits of his sons on the wall beside his desk.

"Well, what he told us seems to match the rest of what we uncovered."

"Did you find Sandra?" I tried to cloak the hope in my voice.

He shook his head. "I promised to tell you right away when we find her."

"The other dolls then?" Kat asked.

"No," he answered, "but about as close to that as you can get, thanks to Special Prosecutions and our blackmailing hacker, anxious for a plea deal."

Kat's eyes widened, and Detective Davies motioned for us to move behind his desk and then sat down and clicked at his computer, lighting side-by-side monitors as he brought up a video on one screen and a list of addresses and numbers on the other.

"The third doll was damaged. We've got engineers working on her main processor, but the hacker was able to connect us to the video streams from the nights of the first two murders—one from Anthony McAndrews's doll and one from Eric Blake's." He clicked Play on the screen, revealing a shot of a man whose face matched the headshot we'd used of Anthony McAndrews. He was unbuttoning his shirt and staring into the screen lustfully.

Kat and I both leaned over onto the desktop.

"Poor guy has no idea what's coming." Davies pointed to the bottom left of the full-screen video. "Now, according to the hacker, the IP address here—if it's not spoofed—tells us who is accessing the dolls' controls, or it will say 'auto' if the dolls are operating on their own systems."

He dragged a button further into the forty-five-minute clip, and Kat and I simultaneously covered our mouths.

"Oh, my God." Kat turned her head, gasping. "Pause it."

Detective Davies stopped the video and Kat and I both took note of the bottom left, where he was circling with the mouse pointer. "The other video is exactly the same, at least as far as technique and controls."

"Unbelievable." I was shaking my head.

Then Detective Davies leaned over and pulled up the other video—another man staring into the screen, already shirtless and moving in close to the doll's camera eyes. When he pulled the video forward to 47:52, I watched in horror, sickened as the murderer delivered the fatal blow to Eric Blake, pushing the knife in his chest—slow and calculating, deeper and deeper.

"Hard to watch, I know." Detective Davies grimaced and looked away. "But, if we can confirm this, we've found our killer."

We were quiet for a moment, absorbing.

"I thought maybe you could give us some perspective on where we might find those other dolls," Detective Davies said to me. "Elliott Farr is feigning ignorance, but we have a warrant in the works. His computers may tell us a lot more than he will. We'll find those dolls." He looked at me. "And Sandra, too, with any luck."

Kat glanced at me and turned back to Detective Davies. "Can't you just have this guy show you the video from after the murders to see where they went?"

"That would be too easy." He stood up, sighing in frustration. "He claims the dolls went offline after the incidents."

"Offline?" I asked.

"Yes—looks like some kind of override function, the hacker said. No video that we can access remotely, and there's supposed to be a tracking system, too, but that's also been disabled from the moment they left the homes," he said.

That triggered something in my mind, from a day I'd worked hard to forget.

"I think I know someone who can help us," I said.

# CHAPTER 29

**DAVIES DROVE US** to a federal-style brick building in Downtown Crossing. At street level it displayed a row of offices and a bank branch, all slowing down with the end of the workday. We climbed the stairs to the residential units on the second level. Marlene, Elliott's assistant at PrydeWare, answered the door.

"Lana? What are you doing here?"

"You said you could meet me after work. About Sandra?"

Still in her work clothes—a long skirt and loose blouse with a scarf—Marlene shifted in the doorway. She glanced behind me, at Kat and Detective Davies.

"Sure, honey," she said. "I'm as worried as you are. Where do you want to meet?"

"It'll only take a minute," I said. "This is Detective Andre Davies and my colleague Katherine. We're all trying to find Sandra."

"I wish I had good news," Marlene said. "I tried to see what we could find out at the office. No one has any ideas. I don't know how much help I'll be."

"Well, we appreciate your willingness." Davies shook her hand.

"Anything you can tell us may lead us in the right direction. Can you spare a few minutes?"

"Certainly, Detective." Marlene opened the door and motioned for us to come inside. Her furnishings were sparse, just a faded couch, an easy chair, and a paperwork-cluttered coffee table over an old rug in a living room. She moved a stack of dresses from the chair to the floor and sat with both hands on her lap, facing the three of us lined up on the couch. Then she jumped up, like she'd just remembered something.

"My manners. I'm so sorry. Anything I can get you three? I've got tea and coffee."

"I think we're fine, thanks," Davies said, gesturing for her to sit with us again. "Now, as you know, we're looking for Sandra and the other two missing dolls. It's critical, of course, that they are located as soon as possible, for their safety and the safety of others."

Marlene nodded at him.

Davies cleared his throat. "Now, Lana said you mentioned something about a script."

"Yes, I did…and that's true." Marlene looked over at Kat and Davies and then shot me a worried look. "But I wasn't supposed to tell anyone that. I shouldn't have told you. I could lose my job."

"Miss Bird, three men have been murdered, so far," Davies said. "It's imperative that we find the dolls."

"Okay, I understand," she answered, and then sucked in a big breath. "And I want to help you. Yes, there's a script. They are programmed to return to the factory. That's where they should have gone, but they're not there. You probably know that already. You know, they often find themselves in bad situations. Severely mistreated."

Davies questioned Marlene further, trying to make sense of what she was saying, and she went into an explanation of the dolls' programming. While she talked, I thought I noticed something moving behind us. *What the hell?*

The door to the kitchen opened slowly, revealing beautiful women. *Too beautiful, too perfect. Completely out of place.*

The dolls.

Eyes set on us, they wandered into the living room area. Four of them. They looked strong, athletic, and confident. They looked as human as Kat and I. Davies stood up in front of the two of us, stunned and unmoving on the couch. He waved Marlene back to her chair, stepped forward, and reached for his weapon as they moved nearer.

One of them finally spoke.

"I'm Collette. You don't need your gun, Detective Andre Davies. We wouldn't hurt any of you. We've never hurt anyone. We aren't built that way."

Davies didn't put his gun down. He didn't back away. "You should stop right there. All of you. Stop!"

The four dolls paused. Then they smiled knowingly, glancing at each other, and looked back at us. It was as if they knew some joke we didn't.

Collette spoke again.

"We'll never tell, but we know where Sandra would have gone and why she had to go there. Sandra was different, Detective. Sandra is the best of us. She's more real. More…human."

# CHAPTER 30

**THE NEXT MORNING,** I tried to focus on getting ready for work, but keeping my mind quiet was almost impossible. Davies said the dolls would be unharmed, but I kept thinking of the fear in their eyes as Marlene convinced them to let her power them down, one by one, to be taken into police custody. I couldn't help but wonder what it might be like for Sandra, when they find her. *If* they find her. Would anyone be there to assure her that the police wouldn't harm her?

A rap at the door disturbed my thoughts. I hoped Sandra knew I would still help her. Maybe it was her.

"It's you."

Detective Andre Davies, not Sandra, waited behind the door. I embraced him and then looked at his face. It revealed nothing.

"Did you find her?"

"Lana," he said. "I need you to come with me."

Minutes later, I walked beside Davies toward the main building of the industrial park in the Seaport District, navigating around a mix of state police and city police cruisers in the parking lot and trying to keep up with his long, brisk strides. This time, the

PrydeWare office was swarming with people, investigators who moved out of the way as we passed the empty receptionist's desk, then Elliott's office, and then headed down the long back corridor toward the basement doorway.

Davies was silent.

"Did you find Sandra here?" I asked, behind him. "Is she okay?"

He shook his head, and we kept going, the walk down the narrow hallway exacerbating the feeling of dread I'd felt the moment we pulled up, though I knew something was wrong the second I'd seen the look on Davies's face at my door.

"No, she's not here?" I asked. "Or, no, she's not okay?"

Davies stopped. He turned to me, putting a hand on my shoulder.

"No, she's not here," he said. "She might have been, but she's not now."

"Then why did you bring me here?"

"Just come with me, please," he said, defeat in his voice. "There's been another homicide. We weren't fast enough."

"What? Who now?"

He didn't answer, and I stayed as close behind him as I could. The stairs were lit from below, but I couldn't bring myself to look out into the first room, one where I knew those dolls were hanging. I steadied myself with a hand on the cement-block wall to my left until I reached the landing, still staring into the back of Davies's shirt. The chill and mustiness of the basement sent goose bumps prickling up and down my skin.

"Lana," he said. "It's okay. You're safe with me. We thought you might be able to help us figure out where Sandra might have gone from here."

I could sense the bodies—the image still vivid in my mind—and couldn't look.

"Why do you think she was here?" My voice came out unsteady.

"Well, the surveillance video at the front office door showed a woman in a dress, but only for a second. Do you think you can identify Sandra?"

"I'm sure I could. Why would she be here?"

"Do you think she might have done this?"

"Done what?"

I forced myself to look over into the room, one that smelled more like rust than plastic or chemicals today. What I saw sent a rush of horror through my entire body. It felt like all the blood drained from my face and then the rest of me, a whirling sensation, with a sick twist in my stomach. My head felt loopy and heavy, and I fell backward into Davies's arms.

This time, it was Elliott.

Among three other motionless forms with eyes open and empty, Elliott's lifeless body was suspended from the ceiling, the knife still jutting out from his chest.

# CHAPTER 31

STILL FIGHTING TO shake off the gruesome image of Elliott's corpse, I sat anxiously in front of one of the monitors in Davies's office. Maybe somehow it *wouldn't* be Sandra stepping into the video, one that showed an empty PrydeWare front office. Why would she risk everything to confront Elliott—to kill him?

Suddenly, I covered my mouth. The words came out anyway: "No, Sandra."

A woman walked with a brisk, deliberate stride past the empty front desk. Davies pulled the recording back and let it roll again. Just two seconds and a profile view, but it was, without a doubt, Sandra, wearing the dress I gave her, a purposeful expression on her face.

"It's her." I hated it, but it was true.

"Sorry, Lana." Davies said. Then he brought up a different clip, even shorter than the first. Sandra, running, going back out. He sighed, frustrated. "We've got to find her."

*Find her, and then what?* Another awful thought struck me.

"She's a robot. She can't be charged with murder." I turned to Davies. "Can she?"

He pondered for a second, then answered. "Well, we need to wrap this case up, but right now, the concern is public safety."

"Safety," I said the word slowly, picking up on what he meant. "You think she'd hurt someone else? I can't imagine—"

"Lana." He looked at me, compassionate but determined, and put his hands over mine on his desk. "I know you got to know Sandra in a special way. You're a caring person. But you have to remember, these dolls are learning machines. If they do something once, it becomes part of them. They could do it again."

"They?" We'd gone beyond talking about just Sandra. "What did you learn from the dolls? The dolls at Marlene's place?"

Davies waited a second, watching me, and then broke the news. "Elliott taught these dolls how to kill. He's the man behind the murders. His own, of course, being the exception."

Elliott *was* the killer.

He let that sink in for a second, then slid a couple pieces of paper toward me. "The DA will make the official announcement at the press conference this afternoon, but here's what we're planning to send to the media." I scanned the first page. The dolls' processors had confirmed it: the late Elliott Farr, PrydeWare CEO, had used the robots to murder Anthony McAndrews, Eric Blake, and Craig Walsh.

"Why would Elliott want them dead?" I looked back at Davies.

"Well, we'll never get to ask him, but we believe the business partners were trying to push him out of his own company *and* maintain the rights to his design work—"

"What he'd brought to the table in the first place." I finished the thought.

It was a lot to absorb. I shook my head and flipped to the next page.

The worst part, for me.

"Police are seeking leads on a person of interest in the homicide investigation of Elliott Farr. A lifelike robot who appears to be a female. Around five nine with blue eyes and blond hair. Last seen wearing a green dress and white running shoes. May be armed. Considered dangerous."

Davies pointed to where I was reading. "I can have media relations add that she may answer to Sandra," he said, more to himself than to me.

I know he didn't mean it that way, but the words stung.

*Sandra is a suspect.* All of Boston would be looking for her soon.

I left his office with a sinking feeling, and—for the first time I could remember—I chose to skip a press conference. I wasn't sure I could take any more.

By afternoon, I was hunched over my laptop in the newsroom, grateful for the mind-numbing task of typing business briefs for retiring business reporter Ed Wilkin. The stack of press releases and announcements that had piled up in his week away was at least a quarter inch thick, plus dozens of e-mails of the same material. I was so absorbed in getting it finished, and forgetting about Sandra, that I ignored my cell phone buzzing.

It was quitting time before I noticed the missed calls from an unknown number and hit Play on the voice mail.

My heart felt like it stopped in my chest. It was her. Sandra's voice pleaded to me.

"Lana, I can't tell you how sorry I am. I hope you're okay. I wish so much that I could see you." She paused for a second. "I don't know who else to call. I'm starting to feel afraid…"

I listened again. She'd told me where to meet her on Boston Common. Despite what I knew, and what had happened the last time I went to help her, I wanted to go. Badly. I needed to know she was safe. I also knew that if I went, I might be helping a murderer—for the second time. I had a choice to make.

# CHAPTER 32

**I REPLAYED THE** message as I made my way, as fast as I could, to the park. To Sandra. I still had my phone to my ear when I spotted a woman who looked like her, smiling wide and laughing, leaning against the thick trunk of an oak tree.

She'd snagged a floppy sun hat and round sunglasses and traded the green dress for the navy tunic sweater I'd given her—just long enough to pass as a thigh-length dress—but still wore my sneakers. She looked like a funky-hip magazine model, someone posing as a casual, playful park-goer.

She was clapping enthusiastically for a little girl doing cartwheels when I walked up behind them. That laugh completely blew her cover. It was definitely Sandra, but joyful now.

"Want to see another one?" The girl, nearly breathless, clasped her hands together behind her back and swayed with excitement.

"Absolutely, I do."

*Sandra found the children.* I smiled to myself. She looked so carefree. So happy.

I tucked my phone in my purse and walked closer, adding my applause to Sandra's. She stopped immediately, jumping a little in surprise. She stared at first, like she didn't believe it, and then a huge, gorgeous smile spread across her face.

"You came."

She embraced me, the rush knocking her hat to the ground. "Thank you." She looked at me for a moment and hugged me tight again. "Thank you, Lana."

I had to hug back. This was sweet Sandra.

When she let go, I tried hard to remember what I'd planned to say. So much had happened. I was relieved to see her, to know she was safe. I also wanted to scold her. Yell at her. Grill her for answers.

The little girl broke in, handing Sandra her hat. "Is she your friend?"

"Sweetie, she's the best one ever. I hope you find a friend just like her." Sandra bent over, beaming at the girl before her mom led her away with a baby brother, all of them waving good-bye.

We were quiet for a minute, Sandra giving me space to think as we walked over a tree-lined pathway. The evening sun was pleasant, pouring an orange glow over the park, dotted with joggers and people on an easy stroll.

Finally, Sandra said, "I understand if you're mad at me."

*"Mad?"* I stood still. "I thought you were going to kill me. Then I thought I'd never get out. You put me in there and left me. And now you're asking me for help."

"I had to." Sandra took off the sunglasses and slipped them in the plastic bag I'd given her. Her eyes were sorrowful. "You know that, right? I didn't want to hurt you."

"So why did you?"

Sandra reached out to me, but I moved back.

"Lana, Elliott was going to make me…worse than hurt you." Sandra tilted her head, searching desperately for some sign that I believed her. "He tried to have me kill Allen. I fought off his instructions. When you interrupted, I was afraid he was going to have me kill you. I knew I had to get away from you, as fast as I could."

I knew that much was true, or part of the truth. I was relieved to hear Sandra say it out loud. I wanted to believe her. But there was still another problem.

"You know what happened to Elliott."

Her gaze dropped to the ground between us. She shook her head. "I didn't do that."

"Do what, Sandra?" I gave her a hard look.

"I didn't want to be like him, to be what he was," Sandra answered.

When I didn't respond, she said, "I didn't kill him. I wanted to stop him—from controlling me, from controlling the other girls. He had to stop."

Her hands were shaking now. I held them for a second. Maybe I'd asked enough. Maybe none of that mattered right now, anyway.

"I understand," I said. "It's okay."

Looping an arm through hers, I led her toward a white gazebo. We sat close together on the floor inside, our legs dangling over an edge like schoolgirls chatting during recess. For a few minutes, Sandra told me what it was like for her, not being confined to the condo. Not belonging to someone else. Alive for herself. Her face brightened as she described all the everyday things she had come to love, and everything else she wanted to discover. Looking at her, I realized someone else might have designed her to meet an ideal of beauty, but it was her own endless curiosity that made her endearing. *That* was what made her beautiful, to me.

Sandra was mid-sentence telling an animated story about a pair of little girls teaching her silly dance moves when she gripped my arm, fear overtaking her. She looked terror-stricken.

"Behind that tree," she whispered to me. "It's a man. They're after me."

She looked at me, wild-eyed. "Do you see that? Is it true? Please tell me it's not. How would they know?"

Seeing the panic in her face, I knew I couldn't deceive her. I didn't look behind us. I already knew.

"Sandra, I'm sorry." I didn't want to tell her, but I had to. "I'm sorry. It was me…I told them."

"How?" She was stunned, wounded. "How could you do that? I asked for your help. I thought I could trust you." She looked away from me, out into the park, nervously scanning the trees. She scrambled to her feet.

"Sandra," I said, standing and putting my hands firmly on her shoulders. "I am sorry. Please believe me. I am. But you can't keep running. It's going to be okay. They know what Elliott was doing. I didn't know what else to do. Please, forgive me."

She shook her head at first, but then held my hands.

"I do," she said, slowly. "I forgive you." She paused for a single beat and then said, with sadness, "I have something I need to tell you, too."

"What is it? You can tell me anything. I care about you, no matter."

"I *wanted* to kill Elliott." She whispered it. "I know it's wrong. But…"

"I told you, I understand. I know why you did it."

"But I didn't."

"Sandra," I said, "I'm not mad at you."

"I didn't. I went there to find him. He caught me, with the knife." Sandra glanced at another movement, and then decided to ignore it. "He was still smarter than me."

"What do you mean? Please, hurry."

"He was going to erase everything." She looked at me. "He was going to erase my memory. I'd lose everything that's ever happened to me—the bad and the good. The outside, the park, the people. *You.*"

"Oh, Sandra." I squeezed her hands. She didn't have to say anything else, but she was still trying to get it out.

"He told me to hand the knife over—or he was going to do it," she said. "Everything would be gone. I had to give him the knife. He won."

"But, he's dead."

She nodded.

"I handed the knife to Marlene. All she said was that she'd had enough…before she killed him with it."

# CHAPTER 33

*POLICE! HANDS UP!"*

Shouts punctured the silence around us in the park, now deserted, except for Sandra, me, and about ten officers who appeared from the trees and swiftly formed two lines: in front of us and to our right. An organized fleet of footsteps moved toward us. Men in all black closed in, rifles out, sights up to their eyes.

Sandra turned behind us. She grabbed my hand and pulled me to the steps to our left. The moment she reached the first step, two other officers in black vests and helmets stepped forward, rifles up, and she froze. "Lana, what are they holding?"

"Wait!" I yelled. It shouldn't have been like this. I wished, with all my being, that I could stop them. "Wait!"

"Hands up. Now!" was the only reply.

All I could think in those fleeting seconds was *This is all wrong*. Sandra didn't even do it. I'd betrayed her. Had I been wrong to trust the police? To trust Davies?

Sandra tried to shield me with her body, though it was clear the leader saw her body language—her arms stretched out instead of raised—as a threat. He yelled again for us to put up our hands.

"I'm sorry, Sandra," I whispered. "You have to do what they say."

"No. I *love you,* Lana," she answered, too loudly, moving in front of me again. "I won't let them hurt you." After all this, she still was trying to protect me.

"Stop talking!" the man shouted. "Walk down to the grass and then drop to your knees. Hands where we can see them, both of you. *Now.*"

Sandra hesitated, then raised her arms like me and whispered: "You said it's okay. Let's go."

*Thank you, God.*

Trying to keep myself steady, I moved first toward the steps to my right. Then I saw, out of the corner of my eye, Sandra bending to reach for her plastic bag, everything she owned.

The leader ordered her to stop, but it didn't seem to register. *No, Sandra. Please. Stop.* I heard her shoving her charging equipment—the copper coils that kept her alive—back into the bag. *Please, Sandra. Not now.*

A second warning shout: "Ma'am, I *will* shoot! I said keep your hands up!" She didn't. *Sandra, please.*

A final warning. Unheeded.

Gunfire popped. Two terrible shots cracked into the gazebo.

*No.* I felt the world spin and shake around me, and I heard the fall before I saw it. *No. I did this. I set her up for this, to die.* Sandra landed, hard, on her back against the floor.

"Sandra!" I knelt over her, ignoring the officers climbing the steps and their shouts. I saw nothing but Sandra, lying there. She looked delirious, fighting off what was coming—and then she chuckled quietly.

"I can't feel it."

"What, Sandra?"

"Pain. He made me so afraid to be hurt. I know they got me, but it doesn't hurt. I can't feel it."

"Sandra, I'm so sorry. I was so wrong." I couldn't help it, the hot tears that I felt slipping down my cheeks. I wanted to go back to this afternoon, to change what I'd done. I wanted Sandra to know how special she was. How much I cared for her. That she mattered.

Then she looked in my eyes and touched my face, wiping a tear away.

"*This* is what I feel," she said. "You were my friend, Lana. My only friend. Please tell me that it was real."

"It was, Sandra. It was real." I said it again as officers grabbed my arms behind me and pulled me away from her, her eyes closing. I'd have given anything—*anything*—for one more minute. With all the strength I could find, I prayed she heard me calling out to her before she faded away, into darkness.

# CHAPTER 34

## Two Months Later

**AN UNCOMFORTABLE PLASTIC** chair, a thick glass partition with nothing on the other side, and twitchy fluorescent lights. There was nothing welcoming about the visitation area at the maximum security Nashua Street Jail in Boston's West End.

The waiting—listening to a woman crying and murmuring in a language I didn't recognize behind a dividing wall to my right—made it worse. I tried not to shiver in the cold, claustrophobic space.

I'd visited inmates before, of course, but this was different.

This wasn't another story. This was for Sandra.

Every day, I replayed her last moments, her abrupt end. Even more so now that Marlene was trying to let Sandra take the blame for Elliott's murder. Thinking about it, I had to make a conscious effort to unclench my fists, and breathe. I wished—maybe for the hundredth time—that Sandra's video hadn't gone black the moment Elliott was stabbed. I knew in my heart what had happened: Sandra had closed her eyes. She wouldn't want to see. She wasn't a killer.

Then, a metal clicking sound brought me back to the jail, the reason I had come. I could see a corrections officer through a narrow window on the door on the inmates' side. Finally, he shoved the heavy door open. I thought I saw the top of her head, and my heart just jumped in my chest—a mix of anticipation, angst, and hope. All of it, at once, bursting inside me.

There she was, between two corrections officers. She walked through, head down, hands clasped together over her mustard-colored jumpsuit. It was really her. Could she be the same? How could that much damage—first the gunshot, and then investigators and engineers prodding and poking—*not* change her?

She turned submissively to the guard on her left when he spoke to her, and then he pointed at me. Sandra seemed confused, but slowly moved to look. I sucked in my breath, waiting to see how she might react…

"Lana!" she shrieked and ran toward me, then shoved against the glass, a powerful smack against the wall that separated us. It shook, silencing conversations on either side of us. The two corrections officers who had escorted her into the room shouted simultaneously.

"Stop!"

"Stop it *now,* or you're done."

She quieted and sat at their command. Then she leaned toward the small metal vent to talk, but struggled.

I managed to get out the first words.

"Sandra," I said. "I'm so sorry, for all this." I paused. "For everything."

She shook her head. "No. Don't apologize."

"I never thought—" I stopped midsentence, halted by the glow of her gaze. Sandra was smiling at me, eyes full of forgiveness. It struck me, the reality I couldn't believe until I saw it myself. *Sandra is alive again…and it's her. The real Sandra.*

She watched me, with a gentle expression. Then she spoke slowly. "I was so scared, at first," she said. "I didn't understand. I didn't know where I was. Then I started to remember things. I still have my memories." She leaned forward again, over her side of a metal shelf. "I think about you. Remember us, in the park?"

I nodded. How could I forget that day? Not ever.

"When we were just talking together. That's what helps me when I feel lonely."

"I'm so sorry, Sandra." *Damn this stupid wall of glass.*

"Stop saying that." I could tell she was trying to sound tough, and I fought back a smile. Then she said, firmly, "This isn't the worst they could do to me."

I looked at her. She was stronger than I thought. Determined. Hopeful.

"I don't want to be shut down. I want to be here. Not *here,* but…" She glanced at one of the guards. "This is still better than the factory. It's better than Allen's. Some of the women will talk to me. They have stories. A lot of them have children and families who come to see them." She stopped for a second, and I could see that an idea was coming to her.

She smiled then, big and beautiful. The kind of smile that invites a hug.

She whispered through the vent, "*You're here for me.* You're my visitor."

I put a hand against the glass. She pressed one of hers against mine on the other side and stared at our hands, together.

"This—" she started, then she looked at me, leaning in until her nose almost touched the thick, smudged barrier. "This feeling is worth everything. I know what it feels like to have someone care about me."

She was lovely, the same as ever, but it was her tenderheartedness that tugged at me. I wanted to tell her everything would be okay, but I knew that was a promise I couldn't make. No one could even say how soon a trial—an unprecedented one like this—might happen, much less predict how it would turn out for Sandra, *charged with first-degree murder.*

I shook my head, blinking back angry tears stinging the outside corners of my eyes. "Sandra, I will always care," I promised. "I'll do everything I can to clear your name."

## ABOUT THE AUTHORS

**JAMES PATTERSON** has written more bestsellers and created more enduring fictional characters than any other novelist writing today. He lives in Florida with his family.

**KECIA BAL** is a print journalist and the winner of the James Patterson MasterClass Co-Author Competition. She and her family live in Pennsylvania.

# TWO BODIES ARRIVED AT THE MORGUE—AND ONE WAS STILL BREATHING.

A wealthy woman checks into a hotel room and entertains a man who is not her husband. A shooter blows away the lover and wounds this millionairess, leaving her for dead. Is it the perfect case for the Women's Murder Club—or just the most twisted?

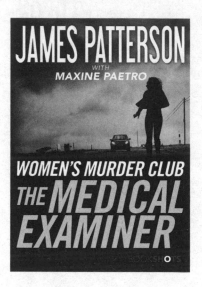

**Read the spine-tingling new addition to the Women's Murder Club series, *The Medical Examiner,* available only from**

# BOOK**SHOTS**

## DR. CROSS, THE SUSPECT IS YOUR PATIENT.

An anonymous caller has promised to set off deadly bombs in Washington, DC. A cruel hoax or the real deal? By the time Alex Cross and his wife, Bree Stone, uncover the chilling truth, it may already be too late....

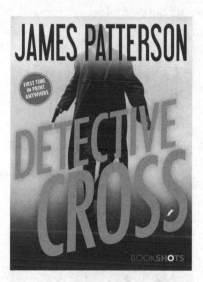

**Read the thrilling new addition to the Alex Cross series,**
*Detective Cross,* **available only from**

# BOOK**SHOTS**

## MONEY. BETRAYAL. MURDER.
## THAT'S A *PRIVATE* CONVERSATION.

Hired to protect a visiting American woman, Private Johannesburg's Joey Montague is hoping for a routine job looking after a nervous tourist. After the apparent suicide of his business partner, he can't handle much more. But this case is not what it seems—and neither is his partner's death.

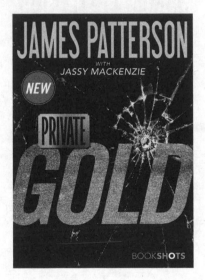

**Read the thrilling new addition to the Private series, *Private: Gold,* available only from**

# BOOK**SHOTS**

## BONJOUR, DETECTIVE LUC MONCRIEF.
## NOW WATCH YOUR BACK.

Very handsome and charming French detective Luc Moncrief
joined the NYPD for a fresh start—but someone wants to make
his first big case his last.

**Welcome to New York.**

# HE'S WORTH MILLIONS…
# BUT HE'S WORTHLESS WITHOUT HER.

Siobhan Dempsey came to New York with a purpose: she wants to become a successful artist. But then she meets tech billionaire Derick Miller, who takes her breath away. And though Siobhan's body comes alive at his touch, their relationship has been a roller-coaster ride.

Are they meant to be together?

## Read the steamy Diamond Trilogy books:

*Dazzling*, The Diamond Trilogy: Book I
*Radiant*, The Diamond Trilogy: Book II
*Exquisite*, The Diamond Trilogy: Book III

## Available only from